"I love Rick," she insisted.
"And I always will!"

"You love a dead man," Jonas said bitterly. "A memory, Sara. A man who can't hold you in his arms...can't make your body tremble with wanting—"

"Stop it! I don't want to hear any more!"

"Why?" he demanded fiercely. "Because it's true? You're clinging to your dead lover because you're afraid to let yourself feel any emotion."

"No! You're wrong." She was almost sobbing.

"Am I, Sara?" He slowly bent his head toward her. Slowly, his mouth moved over hers, his lips lingering, caressing and tasting her with such deliberate languor that she couldn't suppress the moan of arousal low in her throat.

He drew back then, eyes glittering with triumph. "I'll take you home now," he said coolly. "Think of me tonight when you're all alone in your cold little bed."

PENNY JORDAN was constantly in trouble in school because of her inability to stop daydreaming—especially during French lessons. In her teens she was an avid romance reader, although it didn't occur to her to try writing one herself until she was older. "My first half-dozen attempts ended up ingloriously," she remembers, "but I persevered, and one manuscript was finished." She plucked up the courage to send it to a publisher, convinced her book would be rejected. It wasn't, and the rest is history! Penny is married and lives in Cheshire.

Books by Penny Jordan

HARLEQUIN PRESENTS

HARLEQUIN SIGNATURE EDITION

Don't miss any of our special offers. Write to us at the following address for information on our newest releases.

Harlequin Reader Service
901 Fuhrmann Blvd., P.O. Box 1397, Buffalo, NY 14240
Canadian address: P.O. Box 603,
Fort Erie, Ont. L2A 5X3

PENNY JORDAN

too short a blessing

Harlequin Books

TORONTO • NEW YORK • LONDON
AMSTERDAM • PARIS • SYDNEY • HAMBURG
STOCKHOLM • ATHENS • TOKYO • MILAN

The pleasure of possessing
Surpasseth all expressing;
But 'tis too short a blessing,
And love too long a pain

Harlequin Presents first edition November 1987
ISBN 0-373-11023-5

Original hardcover edition published in 1987
by Mills & Boon Limited

CHAPTER ONE

THE moment she stepped inside the front door, Sara Barclay saw the change in her brother. Gone was the morose, withdrawn man she had left behind two weeks ago, and in his place was the older brother she remembered from her teenage years.

'Managed to tame the wild beast, did you?' he teased as he rolled his wheelchair forwards to relieve her of her suitcase.

'Just about.'

The wild beast in question was the very advanced computer-cum-word processor which her brother had just purchased, and which she, as his secretary-cum-assistant, had spent the last fortnight learning to operate. In addition to its basic functions, the machine was so advanced that it could be locked into the information banks of other computers on a worldwide scale, thus enabling Sam to keep himself completely up to date with the economic world. Before the devastating accident which had robbed Sam of the use of his legs and killed both Sam's wife, Holly, and Sara's own fiancé, Rick, Sam had been part of the frenetic world of currency dealing, with a brilliant future ahead of him.

Now that was gone, along with so much else; Sam was virtually confined to his wheelchair, able to walk only a dozen or so steps unaided, his health far too uncertain to permit him to work in the gruellingly demanding world of currency dealing, where young men could be burned out by the time they were thirty, unable to keep up with the ferocious pressure of the work. Sam now worked from home, writing for various economics magazines, and working on the book he was trying to write—a blend of fact and fiction based on the world he had once known.

Getting the computer had been Sara's idea—a last-ditch attempt to rouse her brother from the miasma of depression that had engulfed him since Holly's death, but it was obvious to Sara as he ushered her into the sitting-room of his London house that something had happened during her absence to restore her brother to something approaching his old self.

'Where's Carly?' she asked him as she sat down.

All of them had been affected by the tragedy of the two shocking deaths and Sam's physical disability, but surely the person to suffer the most damage must be her little niece? In one short evening Carly's small world had been virtually destroyed. Her mother had been killed, and her father so badly injured that for days the doctors had despaired of being able to save him.

Perhaps it was no wonder that she and Carly should have grown so close in those early weeks after the accident. Physically Carly had clung to her, but emotionally she had been the one to cling to the little girl, Sara acknowledged. Without the responsibility of Carly, she doubted if she could have found the will to survive those dreadful early days.

Even now, over eighteen months later, they were still etched sharply on her memory: the laughter when Holly set off with the two men to drive them to the station to catch the train for Cambridge—Rick, her fiancé, had been at university with Sam, and it was Sam who had introduced them. Sam and Rick were attending a new computer course together, and she and Rick had been spending the weekend with her brother and his family. She and Rick had been going to be married, six weeks after the course ended.

They had met and fallen in love over a long period of time, but she was still at the ecstatic disbelieving stage, still giddy and delirious with the pleasure of being in love and loved in return.

And then in one short, horror-filled afternoon her whole world was overturned.

She hadn't worried when Holly didn't come rushing back. Her sister-in-law had said that she might take advantage of having a resident babysitter to do some shopping, so when the knock came on the door and she opened it to a white-faced police constable the very last thing in her mind was that there had been an accident.

At first she had been too shocked to take very much in. The first numbing discovery that Holly, lovely, laughing Holly whom her brother adored, and Rick, dear, wonderful Rick, who had made her whole world come alive, were both dead, was so immensely unbelievable that it blotted anything else out.

Scooping up Carly, she had gone numbly into the police car, and from there to the hospital, leaving Carly in the care of a calmly smiling nurse while she was ushered into a room where a grave-faced doctor tried to explain to her why it was impossible for her to see her brother.

After that there had been a week of disbelief,

broken sharply by unbearable bursts of pain; Holly's and Rick's funerals; the shock and despair on the faces of their families. She and Sam had only one another; their father had died from a heart attack when Sara was in her mid-teens, and their mother had slowly faded away after that, dying when Sara was nineteen.

Sara had had a good job as a secretary, which she had planned to give up when she and Rick married. In the circumstances, leaving a little earlier had presented no problems. During those first early weeks there had been a lot for her to cope with. Visits from Sam's employers, Sara's keen perception showing her that beneath their concerned enquiries was an implacable determination to let her know that there could be no place in the company for a man with Sam's disabilities—a man who would virtually be confined to a wheelchair—if he was lucky.

There had been no immediate financial problem—she had her savings to draw on to keep herself and Carly; it was out of the question for her to approach Sam concerning money. He was far too ill to be worried by anything like that.

Even when it was clear that he would survive, the doctors were very reluctant to let him come home. He had had to spend time in a rehabilitation centre, learning how to deal with his lack of mobility, and from there his doctors had wanted him to go into a home until they deemed him well enough to leave, but Sara had insisted that she was perfectly capable of looking after him; indeed, she had fought untiringly to get him home.

After the funeral, Holly's parents had offered to

take Carly, but they were an older couple who, much as they loved their granddaughter, lived a life far too quiet and retired for a lively five-year-old, and so, without making any deliberate decision, Sara had found herself slipping into the role of surrogate mother to Carly, and nurse-cum-companion to Sam. If nothing else, it gave her some reason to keep on living.

Over the last six months Sam had commented on several occasions that she should get out more, make new friends. New men friends, he meant, but that part of her life had gone for ever. Where she had once been warmed by her love for Rick, she now felt cold—dead, really. She had no desire to replace him. A psychologist would no doubt put her lack of interest in men down to the fact that she was afraid ... afraid of loving and losing again, but logic, no matter how well founded, was no opponent for feelings. She had loved Rick and she had lost him, and she could never again be the girl she had once been. Everything about her now was muted and slightly withdrawn. She had become a woman who preferred the cool protection of the shadows to the heat of the sun.

As she sat down in an armchair opposite her brother, her eye was caught by a letter lying on the coffeee table. As she read the letter heading and recognised the name of her brother's solicitors, her body tensed.

Ever since the accident, a long legal battle had been going on between Sam's solicitors and those acting for the man who had caused the accident.

Even now, Sara could not think about Wayne Houseley without her stomach cramping with agony and bitterness flooding her heart.

The first time he approached her she hadn't known who he was. The police had simply told her that the driver of the large, powerful car which had smashed into Holly's small Citroën had been drinking before the accident.

Wayne Houseley was fairly well known as an entrepreneur, and certainly Sara had seen his name in the papers. Sam had been convinced that he was driving the car, and it was later confirmed that he and his wife had been on their way home from a luncheon party, but when the police reached the scene of the accident, Wayne Houseley had informed them that his wife had been driving the car.

There had been no witnesses to the accident, barring Sam, who of course could not be considered impartial ... and although Sara was sure that the police believed her brother, legally speaking it looked as though Wayne Houseley was going to get off any charges, other than that of careless driving levelled at his wife.

Sam's insurance company and solicitors had assured them that financially this would not make any difference—the Houseleys would still have to pay considerable damages, and Wayne Houseley had been properly insured—but it was the man's arrogant ability to avoid any responsibility for what he had done that made Sara bitter. She was convinced that her brother had been right when he said he saw Wayne Houseley in the driver's seat of the large BMW and not his wife, and it seemed to Sara that Wayne Houseley was typical of that breed of men who considered that their wealth and the power it brought them set them above the law.

It was wrong that Wayne Houseley should not be punished, wrong that his wife should be forced into accepting the blame, but then of course his wife had not been drinking . . .

'Houseley wants to settle the damages out of court,' Sam now told her, seeing her frown. 'Jenkins thinks I should accept.'

He watched as Sara's mouth tightened, saddened to see what the last eighteen months had done to his sister. Sara had always been a pretty girl, and now she was a beautiful woman, but one who carried with her a haunting aura of pain. The blue eyes, that once danced with laughter and happiness were clouded and withdrawn; her dark auburn hair seemed to have lost some of its gloss and glow. She was thinner, he recognised guiltily. He had been so wrapped up in his own pain that he hadn't always realised that his tragedy had been Sara's, too.

'I've asked Mrs Morris to look after Carly for the afternoon,' he told her, answering her earlier question. 'I wanted to have a talk with you.'

He paused, and Sara had the impression that he was intensely excited about something. His thin face had a colour she had not seen in it for months, his eyes—the same shade of blue as her own—snapping with the fierce enthusiasm that had once been such an integral part of him, but which had been lost since the accident.

'Look at this.' He picked up a glossy magazine from behind his chair. It was open at the property advertisement section, and a brilliant red circle was drawn round one of the ads. Sara read it slowly.

'For sale—part-Tudor cottage badly in need of

sympathetic renovation in accordance with Grade One Listed Buildings requirements, plus one acre of land and private gardens.'

'It sounds idyllic,' commented Sara idly, 'but it's very much off the beaten track, isn't it?' The address given was in a part of Dorset that Sara knew to be rather remote. As children she and Sam had lived some twenty miles away from the village mentioned, and both of them knew the area reasonably well.

She looked up and and saw the expression in her brother's eyes, her own opening wide as she breathed unbelievingly, 'Sam, you aren't thinking of buying it, are you?'

'Not thinking of it,' he agreed with a grin. 'I've already decided.' He saw her face and added hastily, 'Look, before you start objecting, let me tell you what I've got in mind. I rang the agents up last week and arranged to go down and see the place. I took Phil Roberts with me—you remember, he's an old friend of mine from Cambridge who's now with one of the big London estate agents. I wanted him to check the place over for me, and he was quite impressed. Basically it's pretty sound, although very, very run down. But best of all, it's got enough outbuildings for us to convert them into a ground floor self-contained unit for me,' he grimaced faintly, 'I'm sick of sleeping in the sitting-room, and a traditional bungalow doesn't really appeal, so . . .'.

'But Sam, it's miles from anywhere . . . totally cut off . . . and all that land——'

'It's what I want, Sara,' he interrupted, looking directly at her. 'Holly was the one who liked London, and it was always on the cards that we'd leave one day.

There's nothing to keep me here now. I can work just as easily from Croft End as I can from here—more easily once the new computer's installed. And think of the benefits for Carly—and for you. You always did have a yen for a cottage with roses round the door.'

He was teasing her, Sara knew, but there was a grain of truth in what he said. Their father's job had been one which necessitated almost constant moves, and as a child she had longed for security, for what she had seen as the comfort and protection of a small village atmosphere.

'But all that land . . .' she protested again.

'Not just the land,' Sam told her with a grin. 'A donkey, two cats and a dog go with it.' He laughed when he saw her expression. 'It's quite a story. Apparently the property was owned by a rather eccentric old lady, and she specified to her solicitors that the house was only to be sold to someone who could take on the responsibility of her animals. Apparently she also specified that it was not to be sold to her next-door neighbour—the chap whose land runs adjacent to hers is Croft End's equivalent of the local squire—owns the largest house in the neighbourhood, that sort of thing. He also owns and runs a highly profitable nursery garden, apparently, selling mainly wholesale, and he very much wanted the paddock attached to the cottage to extend his operation.

'I don't know the full story, but according to the estate agents there was some sort of quarrel between him and Miss Betts which led to her specifying that on no account was he to be allowed to buy either the cottage or the land. Apparently the proceeds from the sale are to go to an animal charity. Anyway, no one else seems to be interested—the property isn't cheap, and the alterations won't be either, because of the building being listed, but with the money I'll get from this place I should be able to afford it. There's a huge garden, complete with vegetable plot and fruit bushes; you always did fancy yourself as something of a back-to-nature freak, as I remember! It will be good for Carly, all that fresh country air . . .'

He wanted to go, almost desperately, Sara recognised on a deep twist of pain. This was the first time since Holly's death that she had seen Sam enthusiastic about anything. He wanted her to share his enthusiasm, she knew, but as yet she was too surprised . . . too shocked by his news to know what she felt.

Only one thing was certain. Wherever Sam chose to live, she would be going with him. He and Carly were her only reason for living now. The three of them were a small, very close-knit family unit, and if Sam wanted to bury himself in a remote Dorset village in what sounded like a wreck of a house, then, like it or not, she would be going with him.

Taking a deep breath, she summoned a shaky smile. 'Well, I hope it has electricity,' she warned him. 'Otherwise that very expensive piece of equipment you've just ordered will be no use at all.'

He gave a deep laugh and reached forward to rumple her hair. 'Yes it has, my little pessimist, and not only that, but there's also an ancient generator in the garage. I don't know if it works, but if not I can amuse myself by taking it to bits and then putting it back together again.'

'Yes, minus several parts,' agreed Sara with a grin, remembering the variety of dismembered radios and televisions that had filled their garage at home when they were children. Invariably Sam would be left with several 'parts' over, and yet, incredibly, he had nearly always managed to make the things work.

'I know this has come as a shock to you,' he said quietly, covering one of her hands with his own, 'but I feel in my bones that I'm making the right decision, Sara. I want you to come with us, you know that . . . but if you feel you can't, then Carly and I will still go.'

'I'm coming with you.' She forced herself to sound light-hearted and cheerful as she added, 'When do we actually get to move in?'

'Not for a couple of months yet. I've put Phil in charge of organising the essential work that needs to be done. The property actually becomes ours at the end of the month, and Phil reckons it'll be another couple of months after that before we can move in. Décor and furnishing I'm leaving up to you. Phil is going to come round later in the week with the plans of how it's going to look, and that should give you an idea of what we're going to need.'

'Can't I go down and see it before then?'

Sam shook his head.

'I'd rather you didn't,' he told her with a faint grin. 'It looks so ramshackle that if you saw it in its present state you'd probably refuse point blank to move.'

'But what about these animals?'

'All being taken care of until we actually move in. The two cats are apparently half wild; the dog's boarded out and the donkey is being fed twice daily by a neighbour.'

All in all, she had had an extremely eventful

homecoming, Sara thought later as she curled up under her quilt.

Carly was asleep in the bedroom next door, while she, Sara, slept in what had once been the spare bedroom. No one slept across the landing in the bedroom that had been Sam's and Holly's; Sam slept downstairs in what had been the dining-room, in a specially adapted bed. Although he could do most things for himself, his legs were too weak to allow him to climb the stairs. The accident had not caused any paralysis, but the many operations involved in the rebuilding of his legs had meant that Sam would always have a degree of disability, although in time he should be able to walk, even if he had to resort to his wheelchair occasionally.

As she sank slowly into sleep, picture-book images retained from her childhood mingled with her dreams. A Tudor cottage in the depths of the country. What could be more in keeping with the secret adolescent dreams she had once woven for herself? Dreams that had been upstaged by Rick's emergence into her life, but which were now resurfacing, offering her comfort and something to cling to.

But what about their neighbour-to-be? The local would-be 'squire' whom the old lady had specifically refused to allow to buy her home and land?

Every paradise had to have its serpent, Sara reminded herself drowsily, mentally picturing a heavy, brash male with a ruddy complexion and a manner very like Wayne Houseley's. Did *he* bully his wife the way Wayne Houseley had bullied his? Probably, she thought bitterly. Men of that stamp liked bullying women.

Before Sara finally let sleep claim her, she summoned up Rick's beloved image, a ritual she had performed every night since he had been killed. As always, she felt the enormity of what she had lost consume her, her dry eyes burning more painfully than if she had shed tears.

If only she and Rick had been given more time . . . if only she had his child to comfort her as Sam had Carly. If only . . . The saddest words in any language, surely?

CHAPTER TWO

'Wow! It's terrific, isn't it, Aunt Sara? Just like that jigsaw Gran sent me for Christmas?' Carly demanded enthusiastically as Sara emerged from the driver's seat of the car to stand alongside her. The rutted track which had led from the main road to the front of the house had jolted Sara's small car roughly from side to side, and she grimaced slightly, wondering how long her ancient Mini's suspension would last if it was constantly exposed to the rigours of the cart track. Little wonder that Sam had not seen fit to mention it during his eulogy on the delights of their new home!

Carly was quite right, though: the white plaster-work and black beams of the cottage, and the lavish display of cottage garden flowers in the beds bordering the road, made an ideal picture-postcard scene. A narrow brick path led towards the open front door, the bright May sunshine bouncing off the diamond-paned windows.

Sam had travelled down to their new home the previous day with Phil, leaving Sara and Carly behind to finish cleaning up the house and to check that the furniture removers did their job properly.

The furniture van had not yet arrived, and Sara suspected that its driver would be none too pleased with their cart track of a road. Still, she certainly could not carp at the setting: lush fields, broken up by green clumps of woodland spread all around out on three

sides of the cottage. On the fourth was what Sara
guessed must be the paddock, complete with the
donkey, which had just caught Carly's eye. On the far
side of the paddock was a high brick wall, presumably
the boundary of their land and the beginning of that
belonging to their one neighbour.

Sara had driven through the village before turning
off for the cottage. It was only a mile or so away, but it
seemed a pity that the nearest neighbour had to be
such an unpleasant sort of person. Mentally shrugging
the thought aside, she pushed open the small gate and
ushered Carly up the brick path ahead of her.

Sam was waiting to welcome them inside, and he
was actually standing free of his wheelchair, Sara
noticed with delight, and beaming at both of them as
he stood back to let them get past him and into the
small square hall.

The soft cream walls and exposed beams made Sara
cry out with pleasure. The stone floor underfoot was
worn and polished by time. As yet the hall was
unfurnished, but in her mind's eye Sara saw the floor
covered by the Persian rug Holly had bought the first
Christmas she and Sam were married.

A narrow staircase twisted upwards, light pouring
into the hall from a casement window with a seat just
big enough for Carly to perch on.

'Come into the sitting-room. Luckily everything's
been finished on schedule. Phil told me the builders
were working late every night last week to get it all
done. I must say they've done a superb job. Just wait
until you see the kitchen—complete with Aga, I might
add.'

When consulted about what she would like in the

kitchen, Sara had opted for the traditional fuel-burning cooker, knowing that it could be relied upon to provide both heat and somewhere to cook food should there ever be any problems with their electricity supply. The cottage was too remote to have been supplied with gas, and despite Sam's claim that he could get the generator working, Sara felt that she would prefer not to have to depend on it. Dorset was notorious for its heavy snow-falls, and the last thing she wanted was to be snowed up in a remote cottage without any form of warmth or means to cook by.

'When the builders started work, they discovered this fireplace,' said Sam. 'It was bricked up and hidden behind some plasterboard.'

He stood to one side so that Sara could admire the large traditional fireplace that had been uncovered. As with the hall, the walls in this room had been painted a soft cream, the starkness offset by the dark beams.

The sitting-room was suprisingly large, with windows at either end. The rear windows overlooked the gardens, and Sara wandered over to look out, catching her breath in a gasp of pleasure as she did so.

Beyond the overgrown brick-paved patio area stretched an emerald-green lawn bordered by a wilderness of traditional cottage garden plants. A lattice trellis, broken in places and smothered in roses and clematis, separated the lawn from what Sam told her was the vegetable garden and a small orchard.

'You can explore it all later,' he told her firmly, grinning at her. 'Come and have a look at the rest of the house.'

Thanks to Phil's careful planning, the downstairs of

the house had been extended to incorporate what had once been a motley collection of outbuildings. These now comprised a comfortable sitting-room-cum-study for Sam, a good-sized bedroom, and his own specially organised bathroom.

The extension ran at right angles to the main building, and opening the French windows of his sitting-room, Sam told her that he wanted to extend the paved area of the garden so that he would have somewhere to sit and work during the summer months.

In addition to the sitting-room, the main part of the house also had a very small study, a dining-room and a well-proportioned kitchen. Upstairs there were three bedrooms and a bathroom. One of the bedrooms had obviously been decorated with Carly in mind, but the two others had plain cream walls—so that she could choose her own décor, Sam told her when she rejoined him downstairs.

'It's perfect, Sam,' she told him, laughing when he teased,

'In spite of the cart-track outside? Apparently the guy who owns the property next door wanted to have it made up properly, but Miss Betts wouldn't agree. She liked her privacy and maintained that the state of the lane prevented her from getting unwanted visitors. Jonas Chesney, who owns and runs the nursery, wanted the road made up because his buyers find it difficult to use—especially in winter. It runs right into the back of his property.'

'And considering himself the local squire, he wouldn't want the hoi polloi turning up at his *front* door, of course,' put in Sara nastily.

Sam raised his eyebrows slightly. 'I don't think it's a matter of that. It seems that the greenhouses and his office are close to what used to be the stable block, and that's where this lane leads to. The house itself and the main gardens are open to the public certain days of the week. I haven't seen it myself, but apparently it's a lovely place—beautifully maintained, which can't be cheap. Derek Middleton, Miss Betts's solicitor, had nothing but praise for the man. I get the impression that he thought Miss Betts had behaved very unreasonably towards him. It seems that at one time the family owned all the land around here, but Jonas Chesney's uncle had to sell off most of it to meet death duties. Middleton told me that Jonas has done wonders with the place. It seems he gave up a very promising career abroad to come home when his uncle died, and he's made a real success of this nursery business. He wanted the land to extend into, it seems.'

'Mmm ... I don't suppose he's going to be overjoyed about getting us for neighbours,' said Sara aggressively. 'I expect he'd hoped to get the place at a knock-down price when Miss Betts died. No doubt it came as quite a shock to him to discover the contents of her will.'

'What's got into you?' Sam looked distinctly puzzled. 'Anyone would think you'd actually met the man and taken a violent dislike to him.'

'I know his type,' Sara said shortly.

Sam frowned, his mouth relaxing a little as he said softly, 'Sara, I know what you're thinking, but from what I've heard, he isn't the same type as Wayne Houseley at all. Far from it. A less scrupulous man could easily have found some way round Miss Betts's will, you know, and this morning when I arrived I found he'd sent over a basket of eggs and some milk and bread. I think you're making an unnecessary ogre out of the man. Don't forget he's going to be our closest neighbour,' he added warningly, his voice lightening as he commented, 'and one whose help we'll probably be very grateful for if that jungle out there is as bad as it looks! I found a goldfish pond on the far side of the lawn. We'll have to get something to cover it—a net or something. I don't want to run the risk of Carly falling in. Speaking of my daughter, where is she?' he asked.

'Talking to the donkey,' Sara told him. She glanced round and asked, 'Where are the cats and the dog?'

'Being looked after by our neighbour, apparently. He offered to take charge of them after Miss Betts's funeral. Mmm . . . that sounds like the furniture van. I'll leave you to deal with them. By the way, I've invited Phil to join us for dinner tonight, if that's okay with you?

Sara nodded her head briefly. Whatever her private doubts might be about the wisdom of their move, she could already see an improvement in Sam. He spoke and moved with a much greater sense of purpose—a resurgence of the old Sam she had missed so much during the last eighteen months. It had been frightening at times to realise how much both he and Carly depended on her, and yet she had needed their dependence simply to give her a reason to go on living.

Rick's death had devastated her. Always a fairly quiet girl, she had become totally withdrawn, unable to cope with the cruelty of the loss. Rick had been outward-going and extrovert, and she had loved him to the extent that he had filled her whole world, leaving little room for anyone else. Even now there were times when she could scarcely comprehend that all that vitality had been wiped out. She dreamed some nights that he had come back to her, that she only had to reach out to touch him. Waking up after those dreams was agony.

There had been several occasions recently when Sam had told her that she ought to go out more, to rebuild her life. To find another man, he meant, but Sara did not want another man. She was content with her life as it was. She had Sam and Carly to love and to love her in return, and that was all she wanted from life. She didn't want to love again, if the truth were known. She didn't want the pain of loving someone only to risk losing them. No ... she was perfectly happy as she was.

She'd already met Phil on several occasions. He was pleasant enough and she quite liked him, but if Sam had any matchmaking in mind ...

The sound of the removal van stopping outside galvanised her into action. She hurried to the front door, glad of an excuse to dismiss thoughts that she thought of as too introspective. She didn't like delving deep into her emotions any more. It was too painful. There had been so much pain in her life that now she had almost no tolerance of it at all. It was as though she was so emotionally scarred that she couldn't bear anything touching the wounded area.

As she instructed the removal men she glanced across towards the paddock, checking on Carly. It was an automatic reaction these days, a reassurance to herself that the little girl was safe. How she had hated it when Carly first started school, but she had taught herself to let go, not to pass on to her niece her own fears. Carly enjoyed school, and Sam had already spoken to the headmistress of the small village school she would be attending from the end of the summer holidays. In view of her age it had been decided that there was no point in her starting at her new school until then, when she would do so with children of her own age, since the country school did not start its pupils at four as had the London one she had previously attended.

She had the whole summer in which to enjoy the company of her brother and her niece, to put down roots and let them flourish in the rich country earth. As she glanced at Carly, her attention was caught by the brick boundary wall, the sight of it reminding her of their neighbour.

Sam didn't want her to be antagonistic towards him, she knew that, but even without knowing the man she didn't like him. Illogical, she knew, but it was there.

'Just one more story,' begged Carly, snuggling further down into her small bed.

Where on earth did children get their energy from? Sara wondered fatalistically as she complied with her small niece's request. There was Carly, all bright and bouncy, while she could barely keep her eyes open.

The removal men were long gone; the furniture all in place. Sam was in his study with Phil discussing his plans for the future. Both men had insisted on helping her with the washing up after dinner, and although she had found Phil pleasant enough she had been glad to excuse herself on the pretext of needing to put Carly to bed.

Now all she wanted to do was to go to bed herself. It had been a long day and she was tired out. The cottage was much larger than Sam's London house, and soon she would have to get down to buying furniture and carpets.

She had been so busy that she hadn't even had time to explore the garden, a treat she had been promising herself all day. Sara had a thing about gardens. She had always loved them, and as a child had longed for one of her own, but her parents had never lived anywhere long enough for her to watch the seeds she had sown grow.

The garden was to be her province; Sam had promised her that. In her mind's eye she could already see a productive kitchen garden, and kitchen shelves filled with bottled fruits and jams. Rick had teased her about her dream of becoming a busy country wife; his future lay in the city, and Sara had willingly abandoned her own girlhood dreams to share it with him. But the garden surrounding the cottage was something that would give her life a new purpose, something of her own that she could cherish and nurture. She wanted that—needed it, she acknowledged, as she gently pulled the covers up round her sleeping niece.

In her own room she stood for a long time looking out into the dark silence. No cars . . . no traffic sounds . . . nothing. It was bliss. Tomorrow she would get up early and explore the garden. Suddenly she felt almost childishly excited, full of anticipation she had not felt in a long, long time.

A flash of orange beneath the green of the lily pad caught her eye and Sara bent to look a little closer, childishly delighted to see the fish. It was only half past six, and she had been awake since five.

Unable to deny herself the treat of exploring the garden any longer, she had sneaked downstairs in her cotton nightdress and bare feet, forgetting that the lawn would be damp with dew.

The sky was a bowl of pale blue edged with lemon where the sun was starting to climb; the garden was so still and peaceful.

The fish rose to the surface, searching for food, its round eyes observing her with calm indifference. Sam was right about one thing: they would need to cover the pool with something to make it safe for Carly.

She had resented Sam's decision to uproot them, but now that she had seen the house and the garden, she knew that nothing could drag her away from it. Smiling wryly at herself, she stood up and moved backwards, the breath leaving her lungs as she cannoned into something solid and warm.

'Careful!'

Calloused brown fingers circled her wrist, the shock of the unfamiliar male voice behind her sending ripples of sensation quivering down her spine. She wrenched her wrist free and swung round, anger sparkling in her eyes.

He was standing so close to her that she had to tilt her head quite a long way to look up into his face.

And what a face! she acknowledged on another wave of shock. Lean and tanned, and so totally masculine that she could feel the tendrils of antipathy curling through her stomach. Whoever he was, she didn't like this man; he was far too male and sure of himself. Beneath the lazy mockery, the grey eyes were regarding her in a way that made her skin prickle. He was looking at her the way a man looks at a woman he finds sexually desirable. She was shocked by the discovery. It affronted her that he should dare to look at her like that. Her throat felt tight with anger. Didn't he know that he had no right to look at her that way? She belonged to Rick—Rick, who was dead, and who could never again look at a woman with desire in his eyes.

A searing, penetrating pain engulfed her, making her stumble back from the concern she saw unexpectedly darkening his eyes. His hand came out and she dashed it away, trembling with fury and dislike.

'What is it?'

His voice was low and urgent, his fingers curling imprisoningly round her wrist as she tried to jerk away.

Tension seized her as she suddenly realised her vulnerability. Her cotton nightdress did nothing to conceal her body from him; she had forgotten how inappropriately dressed she was. Hot colour seared her pale skin as she looked up into his face, demanding to be set free, and saw the way he was studying her body. No one, not even Rick, had ever looked at her with such open sexuality. She could almost smell the maleness of him, she recognised on a wave of revulsion.

'Who are you? What are you doing here?' she demanded huskily, dragging her eyes away from his jeans-clad figure. The jeans were old and worn, the check shirt open over his chest and rolled up to reveal powerful forearms roughened by dark hairs.

'I'm your neighbour,' he told her easily, confounding her. 'I saw you standing by the pool as I walked down the lane, and I thought I'd come and introduce myself.'

He was laughing at her now, and Sara felt her skin burn. She hadn't realized she was so highly visable. Anyone could have walked down the lane and seen her standing there.

Almost as though he knew what she was thinking, he added softly, 'Don't worry about it. The lane only goes as far as my property and no one other than me uses it at this time of the morning.'

'I wasn't worried.'

His intimation galled her, all the more so because he had guessed so accurately at her thoughts. That was another intrusion that she resented. He had no right to read her mind so easily; Rick had been the only man she permitted to do that. It was all wrong that this arrogant, over-confident man should be alive and healthy while Rick . . . A sob of resentment rose in her throat. She had felt like this before, but only in the first weeks after Rick's death, illogically resenting that other young men should be alive while he was dead— but that feeling had faded in time. It disturbed her that this man should be the means of resurrecting it, and she glared up at him, willing him to release her and go away.

'Not exactly friendly, are you?' he murmered wryly, watching the emotions chase one another across her face. 'I wonder why?'

'Perhaps because I don't like you,' retorted Sara waspishly.

The dark eyebrows rose. His hair was almost black and very thick. It was also too long, she thought disparagingly.

'Really? But you don't know me, do you?'

His good-humoured amusement increased her sense of ill-usage.

'I don't want to know you,' she told him through gritted teeth, 'and if you would kindly release my arm . . .'

'In a moment.'

He wasn't amused now. In fact, there was a distinctly disturbing glint in his eyes, a warning that his temper was not perhaps as equable as she had first supposed.

He moved towards her, crowding her against the pool so that she could not escape, the fingers of his free hand drifting lightly along her arm. She shivered beneath the light caress, watching his eyes darken with sexual awareness as his head bent towards her.

He was going to kiss her, she recognised disbelievingly, hardly able to understand what was happening. But it was happening. His parted lips were touching hers, coaxing and very, very experienced.

She wanted to reject him and pull away, but frighteningly, her body wouldn't respond to her will. And worse, it did respond to the sexual expertise it was being subjected to.

Her lips seemed to melt and flower against the seductive male warmth of his, rivers of heat flooding through her veins as his arms went round her to draw against his body.

She could feel the hard jut of his hips through the thinness of her nightdress, and the powerful movements of his chest against her breasts as he breathed deeply.

His hands moulded the contours of her back, resting momentarily on her waist and then moving lower as he made a small sound of satisfaction against her mouth.

Rick was the only man with whom she had experienced passion, with whom she had wanted to taste all the heady delights of fulfilment, but he had been snatched away from her before their love had been consummated, and incredibly, shockingly, her body now seemed intent on relieving all the frustrations of that denial with the man who now held her in his arms.

She heard him mutter something against her mouth as his teasing caress turned into a passionate assault, and then he raised his head to look down into her bemused and vulnerable eyes, his own dark with a desire that her body recognised and welcomed even as her mind and heart repudiated it.

'Well, well. It seems both of us got more than we bargained for,' he told her frankly, his voice rough and slightly unsteady.

Too shocked to make any response, Sara could only stare at him, watching in dumb disbelief as he raised one hand from her body to stroke a calloused fingertip along her moist mouth. His other hand still held her against him, and as he traced the outline of her lips he moved against her, making her intimately aware of his arousal.

It stunned her, both that he could be so easily

aroused and that he should make no effort to conceal it. She had been right to tell Sam that she would not like him, she thought feverishly. It was obvious. The casual attitude to sex which his behaviour betrayed was, to her, thoroughly contemptible.

As she opened her mouth to tell him what she thought of him, his hand slid down her body, caressing first her throat and then the smooth curve of her shoulder, pushing aside the wide neck of her night-dress to expose the rounded gleam of her arm.

His mouth touched the pale flesh his hand had just revealed and the words of denial were choked in her throat as her body quivered in response.

His hand moved to her breast, sliding aside the cotton barrier to reveal its pink-tipped fullness to his gaze.

A dark flush of colour flooded his face, his body tense as his fingers cupped the flesh that had previously only known Rick's caress. Mentally she was filled with a sickening sense of defilement, but physically ... Sara caught her breath on a gasp of mingled shock and excitement as the dark head bent towards her breast and she felt the warm mouth take the place of his caressing fingers. The shudder that went through her made her whole body sag weakly against him, every nerve ending concentrating on the intense physical pleasure aroused by the heated movement of his tongue and mouth against her sensitive flesh.

'No ... No ... please don't ...'

The sobbed words were torn from her throat, tears she wasn't aware of shedding lying damply on her skin.

The look in his eyes as he reluctantly released her breast, only to cover the still moist nipple with the caressing heat of his palm, made her shiver violently.

'I want you.' He said it harshly, as though in some way he found the words as shocking as she did, the look in his eyes suggesting that he was as shocked by the violent passion that had errupted between them as she was herself, but she knew that that could not be so. After all he was the one who had initiated what had happened.

'I want you.' He repeated the words in a slurred, unsteady voice, a blank, almost dazed look in his eyes as he pressed his body into hers, his hips moving restlessly against her.

'I want you!'

He said it more softly this time, bending his mouth towards her own, but the brief respite from the sorcery of his touch had been enough to bring Sara back to sanity. She was appalled by what had happened—that she had actually allowed this hateful man intimacies which before had been permitted to Rick alone—and even harder to accept was the fact that part of her at least had actually enjoyed and wanted the heat of his mouth against her skin. And if she was truthful, wasn't there still a nagging ache deep inside her in rebellious response to the frantic movement of his aroused body against her own?

Shocked by this self-admission, she stepped back from him, an expression of disgust curling her mouth.

His eyes focused on her face, the pupils almost black and very brilliant. He looked like someone coming out of a drug-induced stupor, she thought bitterly as she watched shock and recognition of what he had done vie for prominence in his expression.

'I . . .' He shook his head as though trying to clear it, and Sara knew that whatever he was going to say, she didn't want to hear it.

Logically she knew quite well that when he had first kissed her he hadn't meant it to be anything other than a light-hearted caress, a display of male superiority over the female, but whatever his explanation was going to be for the passionate desire that had exploded between them, she didn't want to hear it. No doubt he would find some way of blaming her for what had happened, she thought bitterly as she pushed past him, ignoring his husky demand that she stay as she fled in the direction of the house.

He didn't follow her, and although she told herself that she was glad, a tiny part of her felt something else. Not disappointment, Sara assured herself vehemently as she hurried back to her bedroom.

From her window she had an excellent view of the garden and the fishpond, but she didn't take advantage of it. Instead she sank down on her bed, covering her face with her hands, engulfed by a feeling of self-disgust so strong that she actually felt physically sick with it.

What on earth could have possessed her? The man represented everything she detested; he was in the same mould as Wayne Housely—an arrogant bully, who thought himself lord of all he surveyed and above the law.

And yet, in his arms . . .

She shuddered deeply. *That* had been physical frustration, that was all. She had grieved so deeply emotionally for Rick that she had forgotten that her body must be grieving for him as well.

Until she met Rick she hadn't considered herself a highly sexed person. She had found it depressingly easy to reject the clumsy sexual overtures of her teenage peers. But with Rick it had been different. He had been six years older than her, for one thing; for another, he had been very sexually experienced. He had not tried to rush her into a physical relationship she wasn't ready for, but by the time they became engaged she would have gone willingly to bed with him had he wished it.

It had been lack of opportunity rather than the lack of desire that had preserved her virginity, and she suspected that her body, resentful of the pleasure Rick had promised it, which it had then been denied, had decide to make its displeasure felt.

Uncovering her face, she stood up and, ruthlessly tugging off her nightdress, studied herself in the mirror.

She was slender for her height, apart form her breasts which were lushly full—more full than usual at this moment, surely, her nipples stiff and aching a little, a sensation which was familiar to her from her days with Rick.

That was all it was, she assured herself guiltily; her body missed Rick's passionate caresses and that was why it had responded so eagerly to . . . to someone else.

A deep wave of colour surged up over her skin as she remembered just how eager that response had been, but she hadn't been alone in that almost frenetic flood of desire. He had been gripped by it too. Instinctively she sensed that he wasn't a man who normally gave way so easily to physical desire. He was the sort of man

who would always want to be in control, she thought
intuitively, both of himself and of the situation he was
in. She hadn't been mistaken, surely, in the shock and
surprise she had seen in his eyes? Or had it simply
been her over-passionate response that had caused his
reaction? she wondered uneasily, her skin suddenly
feeling extremely hot.

Snatching up clean underwear, jeans and a top, she
hurried into the bathroom.

It was half past seven. Carly would be waking up
soon; Sam would want his breakfast. All she could do
was put the incident behind her and forget about it.

But that was easier said than done, when her flesh
continued to tingle disturbingly despite her attempts
to ignore it.

It was galling in the extreme to have to admit that
she had been aroused to such an extent by a man who
was a complete stranger, even if that desire had been
caused originally by her body's physical loss of Rick.

Up until now she hadn't given any thoughts to the
physical aspect of her loss, or to the fact that she
intended to spend the rest of her life without a lover,
and now, suddenly, all her bitterness and resentment
was focused on Jonas Chesney.

What right did he have to be alive when Rick was
dead ... to touch her and arouse her in a way that
Rick no longer could? A sob tore from her throat as
she pulled on her clothes. She hated him, loathed him
... and if she ever saw him again ... But she would
take care that she didn't, she decided grimly. He was
not going to get another opportunity to catch her off
guard as he had done this morning. No doubt he was
already gloating over his conquest of her, she decided

bitterly, conveniently forgetting that not ten minutes before, she had been acknowledging that he was as stunned by what had happened as she was herself.

No doubt it was a favourite hobby of his, to go round collecting female scalps. With those undeniably good looks, and that healthily muscled masculine body ... Swiftly she checked her thoughts, resenting the admissions her body had forced upon her. So he was good looking—so what? That didn't alter the fact that she detested and loathed him.

Perhaps she had been wrong about him, a traitorous inner voice whispered. Perhaps he wasn't another Wayne Houseley after all?

What did it matter? her mind demanded bitterly. He was alive and Rick was dead, and she resented and hated him for that alone.

CHAPTER THREE

SARA was in the sitting-room later that morning, crouched down on all fours trying to measure the floor for new carpets, when she heard a vehicle draw up outside.

Frowning, she turned round to glance out of the window, her body freezing with shock and dislike as she recognised the man clambering easily out of the rather battered Land Rover.

Luckily, Sam was in the front garden chatting with Carly, and would unwittingly delay their visitor.

No doubt it was the same spirit of curiosity that had prompted him to clamber over their hedge this morning which had brought him round now, thought Sara nastily as she hurried into the kitchen, snatching up her handbag and car keys as she did so.

It wasn't as though she was doing something she hadn't planned to do anyway, she reassured herself as she slipped the car into gear and slowly drove out into the lane. She had already mentioned to Sam this morning that she needed to stock up the kitchen cupboards. He had supplied the information that the village boasted only one very small all-purpose shop, and that her best bet would be to drive into Dorchester itself.

The town was a good twenty miles away—plenty far enough for their visitor to have taken himself off long before she returned, Sara thought, pleased by the adroit way in which she had avoided meeting him. Common sense told her she couldn't go on avoiding him for ever, but if he thought that what had happened this morning meant that she would welcome further sexual advances from him, he was very quickly going to be disabused of that idea, she decided grimly, gritting her teeth as her car bumped uncomfortably down the rutted road that was dry after several weeks without any rain.

The sun had risen enough to be hot now, and once she had gained the main road she paused to roll back the roof of her Mini. To her left lay the village through which she had driven the previous day—and to her right? She frowned slightly, noting the massed trees and red-bricked wall. Beyond them lay Jonas Chesney's house. What was it like? That was something she was not likely to discover, nor should want to, she told herself firmly as she turned the car in the opposite direction.

That life in the country proceeded at a somewhat slower pace than it did in London was brought home to her as she did her shopping. Even in the large supermarket, the girls on the till took time to chat to those who were obviously their regular customers. Once she had accustomed herself to it, it was rather pleasant, reflected Sara as she loaded her purchases back into her trolley and wheeled it out to the car.

She was in no hurry to rush back, so she spent a leisurely half-hour wandering round Dorchester, buying some magazines and books for Sam and herself and a story-book tape for Carly. It was well after lunchtime when she eventually set off back stifling her pangs of guilt as she left the carpet shop with a book of samples tucked under her arm.

There was still some salad and cold meat in the fridge. Sam would have been able to knock up a meal for himself and Carly, and she would make it up to them tonight. For a treat she had bought some fresh salmon—too much, really, but what they didn't eat, she could always freeze for a later date.

It was much hotter as she drove back through the country lanes; the hedgerows were green with spring leaf, and ragged robin and ladies' lace mingled patches of deep pink and white by the roadside. She had the road to herself, and with the top rolled back and the windows down she could actually hear the birdsong.

As she headed back home, her earlier tension lifted; she could even mock herself a little for her slightly ridiculous flight from Jonas Chesney. What could the man do to her, after all? All that panic over a kiss. It had been so long since any man had kissed her that she had quite naturally over-emphasised the effect he had had on her.

By the time she turned off the main road into the rutted lane she was feeling pleasantly relaxed and calm, a feeling which disappeared as she swung round a bend and had to brake hard to prevent herself colliding with the Land Rover slewed arrogantly across the road, preventing her from getting past.

Although she wasn't yet sufficiently familiar with her new habitat to recognise one Land Rover from another, she guessed immediately to whom this one belonged. With her heart pumping at something approaching twice its normal rate, she got out of her car and hurried angrily towards the Land Rover. How dared he leave it there like that? Had he no thought for others ... no consideration? No doubt while the cottage had been empty he had got used to considering the road his private property.

The resentment and anger that had fuelled her impatience exploded into furious disgust as she rounded the Land Rover and then came to an abrupt stop, almost unable to belive what she was seeing.

Jonas was half kneeling, half crouching on the far side of the vehicle, the wriggling body of a small boy face down across one hard thigh. Momentarily too shocked to do or say anything, Sara was freed from her temporary stunned paralysis as one calloused hand descended on the boy's jean-clad rear end.

Sara didn't stop to think or to check her words, her horrified, 'Stop that at once!' causing the hand to pause in mid-air.

As Jonas turned a grim and unrepentant face towards her, the child took advantage of his momentary lack of concentration to wriggle free and dart off into the trees at the side of the road.

Swearing briefly, Jonas stood up and, fearing that he was going to pursue the child, Sara grabbed hold of his forearm, her eyes snapping with anger and disgust.

'Don't you dare go after him, you bully!' she said fiercely. 'I ought to report you to the police for what you were just doing.'

'Go ahead,' she was told bitingly, the grey eyes arrogantly disdainful where they should have been guilty. 'I'm sure Sergeant Rowson would be most grateful to you.'

The sarcasm in his voice grated on her nerve endings. Staring up at him, Sara suddenly became aware of the fact that her fingers were still clenched round his arm. His skin felt warm and firm, the dark hairs sensually rough against her palm. She had the most extraordinary desire to let her fingertips stroke along his skin. Releasing him as though his flesh burned, she stepped back from him with flushed cheeks.

'Why were you hitting that child?' she demanded breathlessly, hearing the weak unsteadiness in her voice, and resenting him for causing it.

His mouth curled disdainfully as he drawled, 'Firstly for trespassing on my land . . .' He watched as the indignant colour burned her skin, and then stopped the impulsive protest trembling on her lips by adding, 'but most importantly for this . . .'

He kneeled down again, his lean hands parting the thickly luscious grass with a gentleness that was oddly in contrast to the determined way he had been punishing the boy.

Puzzled and apprehensive, Sam looked down, her stomach tensing as she saw the small cluster of eggs lying on the grass.

'Robbing birds' nests isn't something we approve of round here,' he told her grimly. 'That young lad just happens to be Sergeant Rowson's nephew. His parents have recently been divorced, and the Sergeant and his wife are looking after the boy for a while. He's been city born and bred, and naturally he's having some trouble adjusting. This isn't the first time I've caught him doing this. Last time I warned him what the punishment would be. I wasn't doing it for the pleasure of it, you know,' he told her with a grimace of disgust. 'But the boy needs to know that rules have to be obeyed.'

'I can understand that,' agreed Sara stiffly. 'But you're not related to him; why not leave it to his uncle to punish him?'

'Because by the time I'd found and told the Sergeant and he had got round to dealing with him, the boy would probably have forgotten what he was being punished for. I don't believe in torturing kids with the threat of punishment to come,' Jonas said bitingly, 'whatever you might choose to think. Besides, punishment on the scene of the crime is invariably more effective. The first time I caught him stealing eggs I explained to him just exactly what he was doing, and I had hoped that would be enough. Obviously it wasn't.'

He saw her face and smiled sardonically. 'That doesn't suit you at all, does it?' he mocked. 'You'd much rather see me as the villain of the piece, the sort of man who enjoys inflicting physical pain.' He grimaced slightly and came towards her, saying softly, 'I thought this morning that I detected a certain amount of animosity towards me, cerebrally, at least. Well you know what they say about giving a dog a bad name, don't you?'

She was in his arms before she could move, her brain too dazed to comprehend what had happened. She shuddered as his hand cupped her jaw, tilting her face up to meet the hard pressure of his mouth, her body knowing that he was going to kiss her before her mind could assimilate the knowledge.

Shockingly, her pulses quivered frantically at the first touch of his mouth.

He was kissing her in anger, Sara recognised, making her take the place of the boy she had unwittingly helped to escape, but something was going wrong, because although his mouth was hot and hard, it wasn't anger but passion that fuelled its aggressive demands on her own, and, horrifyingly, she was responding to it. A thick moan was stifled in her throat as his teeth bit sharply into the fullness of her lower lip, tugging on it so that his tongue could touch the inner softness of her mouth. He pushed past her firmly closed teeth as she was forced to draw breath, unleashing a dark need in her that couldn't be controlled by reason.

Helplessly, Sara clung to him, shocked to discover that her arms were round his neck, her fingers clutching at his hair, her body pressed intimately along the length of his.

The kiss went on and on, her lips clinging hotly to his, her tongue powerless to resist the erotic sucking motion that drew it into the heat of his mouth.

A terrible weakness made her tremble against him, the sound he made deep in his throat as he tugged her shirt out of her jeans and slid his hands against the bare skin of her back distantly touching her consciousness.

His heart slammed erratically against his ribs, its unsteady beat driving into her own body, his legs parting so that he could cradle her against the aroused heat of his thighs as he leaned back against the bulk of the Land Rover.

His mouth left hers to explore the pale column of her throat, his fingers deftly unfastening the buttons of her shirt.

She knew she ought to stop him, but the effect he was having on her was too overwhelming, the shock of what was happening to her so immense that she couldn't bring herself to believe it was real. This couldn't really be her, standing in plain sight of anyone who happened to walk past, allowing a man she neither liked nor really knew to practically tear the clothes from her body with one hand while the other gripped her hip and crushed her possessively against the pulsing force of his body!

While Sara's brain fought to comprehend what was happening to her, her treacherous body was awash with the erotic pleasure of Jonas's hand against her breast as it slid inside her shirt and cupped her silk-covered fullness.

She gasped and shivered at the sensations his touch aroused, feeling her nipples tighten and thrust against the frail barrier of her bra. Her head fell back beneath the pressure of Jonas's mouth on her throat, hot and demanding as it found her fluttering pulse.

His own shirt was half unbuttoned, and somehow her hands were inside it, feverishly stroking the moist heat of his skin. His mouth seemed to burn where it touched her, moving hotly along the line of her open shirt. A shudder of physical need convulsed her stomach as his thumb probed roughly at the edge of her bra. Her body's fierce ache to experience the sensation of his mouth against her breast obliterated everything else.

When his impatient fingers finally freed the taut arousal of her nipple, exposing it to the hungry demand of his mouth, Sara wasn't sure which of them made the hoarse cry of satisfaction that reached her shocked ears.

Her brain, trying to come to terms with what was happening, logged with shocked disbelief that the compulsive way in which Jonas's mouth tugged on the swollen softness of her breast was not the sort of caress one would expect from a mere acquaintance. His hips moved rhythmically against hers, drowning out her brief moment of lucidity, and as his hands moved impatiently down her body, holding her fiercely against him, she experienced a shatteringly intense desire for much more than the frantic movement of his body against hers. She wanted him inside her, she acknowledged shakily. She wanted him deep within her with a primitive urgency she had never experienced with Rick.

Rick!

Reality splintered through her fog of physical desire, making her wrench away from Jonas's hands and mouth with a shocked cry of outrage.

She could hear the harsh unsteadiness of his breathing as she fumbled with her shirt buttons, her face brilliantly flushed as the enormity of what she had been doing engulfed her. Totally unable to look at him, she hurried back to her car on dreadfully unsteady legs, disgusted and humiliated by her incomprehensible response to him.

She heard him call out to her, and panicked into turning round and cry out to him, 'Keep away from me, do you hear? Just keep away from me!'

She got into her car without waiting for his response, reversing it awkwardly and driving away. She didn't stop until she had driven through the village, drawing up then in a lay-by and stopping the car, burying her head against the steering wheel as she fought for self-control. It was a good fifteen minutes before she could bring herself to turn round and drive home.

This time there was no sign of the Land Rover in the drive. Sam greeted her with a warm smile when she went inside, coming into the kitchen to help her unpack the food. She felt so jumpy and tense that she felt sure he must comment on it, but, to her relief, he said nothing.

He was putting the salmon in the fridge when he stunned her by saying, 'Good, we can have this for dinner tonight. I've invited Jonas and Vanessa to join us, by the way.'

'Vanessa?'

'Yes. She's Jonas's sister—well stepsister really. I met her the first time I came down here. You'll like her . . .'

Sara wasn't listening. Jonas was coming to dinner. Jonas was coming here. She couldn't stand it. She shuddered, remembering how he had touched her. How on earth could she face him?

How on earth could she not? her pride demanded. She *had* to face him, to let him see that what had happened between them meant absolutely nothing to her. Her almost frantic response to him was the response she had ached to give Rick in the long months since his death; it had nothing to do with Jonas as a person. She closed her eyes, her skin suffused with hot colour as she remembered the way he had touched her . . . the way she had responded.

His passion had been born of anger, hers . . . Hers

had been born of anger too. Anger and loss. It had been no more personal than had his physical desire for her. Somehow telling herself that, made her feel better about the whole thing. It hadn't been Jonas her body had responded to it, it had been Rick. That was the logical explanation. The *only* explanation, she told herself firmly.

It amazed her that she was still able to do such mundane things as prepare food and talk to Sam about the rival merits of the carpet samples she had brought home while ninety per cent of her brain was struggling to blot out completely what had happened earlier in the afternoon.

She tried to tell herself that Jonas had simply been using on her the same tactics he had no doubt employed successfully on numerous other women, but something refused to let her believe this comfortable fallacy. Oddly enough, it would have been more comforting to persuade herself that Jonas had kissed and touched her with a casual expertise that was wholly clinical and given over to nothing more than gaining another female conquest, but her intuitive feminine intelligence stubbornly refused to let her believe such a reassuring piece of fiction. There had been something about the way he held her; something about the almost compulsive need she had felt in him that frightened her much more than mere sexual domination. While logic struggled to deny it, she was conscious of a primitive thread of fear woven from a deeply instinctive belief that Jonas wanted much more from her than she was prepared or able to give.

She had seen and registered the stunned shock in his eyes when he kissed her this afternoon. He had been as caught off guard by the passion exploding between them as she had herself.

Telling herself she was being too imaginative, she went into the garden to look for Carly.

The brick patio just outside the French windows was overgrown and neglected, and she bent absently to pluck out some of the weeds. They came away easily, a satisfying sensation that she wanted to prolong.

A tiny pink flowering plant ran rampant over some of the bricks, and she hesitated as she looked at it. Weed or flower? She ought to have bought herself a gardening book this morning. She had fully intended to, but she had forgotten.

As silkily as a serpent, the thought slid into her mind that Jonas would know. Dismissing it, she got up and hurried across to the paddock where Carly was talking to the donkey. A placid, good-natured child, Carly made no demur when she was told that she would have to go to bed early as her father was expecting guests. Sam oversaw her bath and preparations for bed, while Sara got on with the meal.

The mahogany table and chairs which had initially belonged to their parents and which Sam and Holly had inherited looked at home in the beamed dining-room. Sara had managed to unearth an old lace tablecloth, dulled from its original white to a soft cream that matched the walls, which she remembered as belonging to her grandmother, and the delicate lace-edged linen set off the silver and china Sam and Holly had been given as wedding presents very well.

She had been rather dubious about using them, not wanting to hurt Sam by reminding him of Holly, but when she had tentatively started to get out their everyday crockery he had frowned and asked why she wasn't using the Royal Doulton. She had to admit that the rich dark green and gold pattern looked lovely against the tablecloth; she only hoped that the meal lived up to the elegance of the plates. It was just as well she had brought the salmon, otherwise they would have been reduced to giving their guests beefburgers and salad.

Her mother had been an inventive cook, and she had passed on her love of cooking to Sara. She had made a special sauce for the salmon and a soufflé topping, adapting the ordinances of *nouvelle cuisine* cooking to provide a meal that would both look and taste good.

'That looks lovely,' Sam told her, wheeling his chair into the dining-room while she was putting the finishing touches to the table. Flowers from the garden had provided an attractive centrepiece, and Sara stood back to study her handiwork, frowning a little critically.

'You're a real old-fashioned girl at heart, aren't you?' Sam teased her with brotherly affection, waving his hand in the direction of the table. 'You've inherited our mother's gift for homemaking, Sara.' His eyes held hers as he added sombrely, 'At the moment you're living in a vacuum, but one day I hope you're going to find a man who can give you a home and children of your own.'

'I have a home here with you,' Sara reminded him tersely. 'I don't want another one.'

She looked away from him as she spoke, biting her

lip as she recognised the bitter resentment in her voice.

'I can't replace Rick,' she told Sam huskily, 'and . . . I don't want to.'

'He wouldn't want you to spend the rest of your life alone, Sara. You're only twenty-five . . .'

'You're only thirty,' she said coolly.

'Yes, I know. But, unlike you, I haven't cut myself off from the rest of the opposite sex because of what happened to Holly.'

Stunned by his statement, Sara looked at him with shocked eyes. She had thought that Sam felt as she did . . . that he could never ever feel for someone else what he had felt for Holly, and that, like her, he wanted nothing more than their fraternal relationship and the love they both shared for Carly.

'You mean you would marry again?' Her voice whispered past dry lips, her eyes huge with shock and disbelief.

'If I found the right woman, yes, I would. I'm not a monk,' he told her hardily, 'and Holly wouldn't want me to live as one. I can't replace what I shared with her, and nor would I want to, but that doesn't mean that I can't love someone else—in a different way.' He frowned and glanced at his watch. 'Jonas and Vanessa will be here soon. I'll finish off in here; you go upstairs and get changed.'

Get changed? Sara stared down at her jeans and shirt uncomprehendingly, her eyes swivelling unwillingly to her brother's lean body. Sam had changed into a white shirt and a pair of black trousers. Suddenly she felt terribly alone, as though in some way he had abandoned her. Blinking away stinging tears, she went upstairs and opened her wardrobe doors. What on earth should she change into? She stared blankly at her clothes. It had been eighteen months since she bought anything new. The last semi-formal dress she had bought had been chosen with Rick in mind. She had bought it to go to his firm's annual 'do', but he had been killed before it took place.

Her fingers felt stiff and clumsy as they touched the soft silk, jumping away from the disturbing contact with the sensual fabric. When she had bought this dress she had been a very different woman from the one she was now. It was a wrap-over style, stylish but unmistakably sexy—the sort of dress a woman bought to wear for a man.

Shuddering, she pushed it out of sight, dragging off its hanger a plain black linen dress. The same dress she had worn for Rick's funeral, she recognised numbly, letting it fall to the floor.

She could remember buying it in minute detail, but up until this moment she had almost forgotten she had got it. It must surely be some macabre hitherto unrecognised tendency towards masochism that compelled her to put it on. She wasn't going to listen to that distressingly uncompromising inner voice that said she was wearing it for protection against Jonas, that she was wearing Rick's funeral black like a suit of armour. Zipping up the dress, she studied her reflection with detached interest. Black had always suited her, but since she had lost weight it made her look almost ethereal. She found a pair of court shoes at the bottom of her wardrobe and slipped them on, quickly applying fresh make-up. For some reason it seemed that Sam wanted her to dress up.

She couldn't escape the suspicion that he was trying to do a little discreet matchmaking, hence the pep talk earlier about putting the past behind her. But she didn't *want* to forget Rick, she thought fiercely; she had loved him. Had loved? Still loved, surely? Of course she did. Rick had been her whole life. All that had been left since his death was the shell of the woman she had once been. All? Hot colour crawled over her skin as she remembered the wild passion with which she had responded to Jonas's touch. Shuddering, she put down her lipstick and went into Carly's room to check on the little girl.

She was fast asleep, lying on her side, with one small starfish hand under her pink cheek. Her face softening, Sara bent to kiss the small forehead.

CHAPTER FOUR

'THAT was the most delicious meal! You must let me help with the washing up.'

Vanessa Chesney was nothing like her brother. Petite and blonde, she exuded an air of willingness to please that had instantly made Sara feel protective towards her. It amazed her that a woman of her own age could remain so open and vulnerable to hurt. Vanessa had all the engaging warmth and genuineness of a small child, and like a small child she seemed almost achingly anxious to gain other people's approval.

Once they were away from the men in the kitchen, a little of her anxiety seemed to drop from her, but Sara was still left with the impression that Vanessa considered herself in some way inferior.

'You're a marvellous cook,' she praised Sara as she watched her prepare the cooker. 'I'm afraid I'm worse than useless. Jonas is the domesticated one. I think he only puts up with me out of a misplaced sense of duty——' she grimaced ruefully. 'Not that he ever lets me see it. I doubt if there are many women lucky enough to be able to depend on their brother to provide a roof over their heads and a job. Oh, and that reminds me, we've still got Miss Betts's cats and the dog. Jonas said to tell you that you can come and pick them up whenever you're ready.'

'Jonas has been looking after her animals?'

Vanessa seemed perplexed by her shock.

'Oh, yes. And he's been feeding Fred—the donkey.' She made a face. 'He used to keep an eye on Miss Betts before she died—but very discreetly, of course. It seems such a shame to think that she and Uncle Henry could have been so happy together. It was just her pride that kept them apart. They were engaged,' she enlightened Sara, 'but they had a quarrel—I don't know what it was about, I doubt if anyone does, and she broke off the engagement. Since neither of them married anyone else, Jonas and I can only suppose that deep down they still loved one another. Poor Jonas: the last thing he wanted was to inherit Uncle Henry's house. You should have seen the state it was in! Some of the rooms were damp, it needed re-wiring—the lot. It had been terribly neglected. The parents thought he would sell. We call them 'the parents' because we both have one,' she elucidated with a shy smile. 'Jonas's father married my mother when I was ten and Jonas was fifteen. It was very difficult at first for all of us. My parents were divorced and I bitterly resented anyone else taking my father's place, and Jonas had lost his mother in a particularly horrific air disaster. Sam . . . your brother, has told me about his wife and your fiancé, so I know you'll understand when I say that both Jonas and I hated the thought of someone else taking the place of the parent we had lost. When you add to that the guilt one naturally feels when one discovers the hated step-parent is really a rather nice person, you can imagine the difficult time we gave our natural parents for the first years of their marriage.' Vanessa smiled. 'However, we all managed to weather the storm; I think it's a sign of dawning maturity to be able to accept that one can love a step-parent without being disloyal to the blood parent whose place they're taking. Jonas was better at adapting than me. He was also very good to me. When he went to Canada after finishing agricultural college, I was devastated. The parents never really expected him to come back. He landed a top job over there, managing a huge farm for a large corporation, and when we heard that he'd inherited the house here we all expected him to put it up for sale.

'It hasn't been any sinecure for him, making it pay; he's built up the nursery business from nothing, and the profits he makes on that plus the money he invested from the sale of the remaining farm land just about keeps his head above water, although he says he'll never be a wealthy man. When I ask him why he dosen't sell he says that he feels he can't—that he feels Uncle Henry didn't leave the property to him to sell but to preserve. Of course the house is lovely, and Jonas has managed to pick up some beautiful antiques for it.' Vanessa paused to draw breath and flushed a little. 'I'm sorry if I'm rattling on; I'm too inclined to chatter on like a magpie when I'm nervous. I had quite a bad stammer when my mother married Peter, but he was so gentle and patient with me. Jonas's father is a botanist and naturalist,' she added informatively. 'He and my mother live in a remote cottage in the Fens. I suppose it's from his father that Jonas inherited his love of the land, although he has a far more dynamic personality than Peter. I take charge of the office work, although Jonas oversees the financial side of things. Do you think you're going to like living down here?'

There was just enough wistfulness in her voice to make Sara reply honestly. 'I'm loving it already,' she told her with a quick smile. 'And so is Carly.'

'Carly. I'm looking forward to meeting her. Sam adores her, doesn't he? Is she very like her mother?'

'No . . . not really. If anything, she looks more like Sam. She has his personality, too,' Sara said thoughtfully. 'I could bring her over with me when I come to collect the animals if you like?'

'Oh yes, please do.'

The coffee was ready, and, deftly putting it on the ready-prepared tray, Sara headed for the kitchen door, pausing while Vanessa opened it for her.

In their absence the two men had moved into the sitting-room, and seemed to be deeply engrossed in a discussion about cricket when they walked in. Jonas got up immediately, coming to take the heavy tray from her. His fingers grazed hers briefly, the momentary sensation of skin against skin shocking through her.

Sara deliberately hung back to pour the coffee, keeping herself outside the general conversation. She didn't want to talk to Jonas. She didn't want him in her home, or in her life; she hadn't wanted to hear what Vanessa had told her about him. She preferred to retain her initial, totally erroneous belief that he was a man she could quite easily despise. It was as though she dared not let herself admit she could have been wrong in any way about him, because in doing so she would in some way make herself vulnerable. But to what?

It was a question her mind balked against answering.

As she handed round the coffee cups, she noticed that Vanessa and Sam were sitting close together on the settee, Vanessa listening earnestly while Sam expounded at length about his work.

'Stop boring the poor girl,' Sara scolded her brother as she gave him his coffee. 'I'm sure she's not the slightest bit interested in economics.'

'Oh, I am!'

As Sara looked at her in surprise, Vanessa flushed and bit her lip.

'What my sister is too modest to tell you,' drawled Jonas lazily, getting up from his chair and coming across to join them, 'is that she got a very creditable First herself in Economics. I'm afraid her talents aren't used to their fullest extent working for me.' As he spoke, he leaned over and ruffled Vanessa's blonde hair affectionately, in much the same way as Sam was wont to caress her, Sara recognised.

Sam himself was eyeing Vanessa in much the same light as a miser discovering a hidden source of gold. His eyes lit up and he put down his coffee untouched.

'I think we'd better leave them to it,' Jonas murmured against Sara's ear, as she stepped back from them. 'Unless of course you're the type of sister who doesn't want her brother involved with any female bar herself?'

'Don't be ridiculous.' Sara knew she she sounded terse, but his comment made her feel angry. She had never been the slightest bit jealous of Sam's relationship with Holly, but it was strangely painful to recognise that, unlike her, he seemed ready to put the past behind him and start living again. There had been a very definite glint of male approval in the way he looked at Vanessa.

'Good. Let's leave them to it then, shall we?'

His fingers curled round her arm, making her flinch.

'You shouldn't wear black; it doesn't suit you,' he told her carelessly as he drew her inexorably towards the open French window. 'It's too funereal.'

Sara felt the colour drain from her skin, and she shivered in the light breeze from the open door.

'Sam says you're very keen to start work in the garden. Walk round it with me and tell me what you plan to do.'

As on the previous two occasions when she had met him, Sara found herself struggling against the formidable male power of his will. Jonas frightened her in a way that had nothing to do with his far greater physical strengh; it was a fear that sprang from the terrible vulnerability she sensed within herself towards him. And yet what was she frightened of? The potent sexual chemistry that existed between them? Of betraying the love she felt for Rick by . . . By what? Falling in love with Jonas? There was no way that could ever happen; she didn't even like him—loathed him, in fact.

'I'd rather stay here, if you don't mind?'

They were both talking too quietly to be overheard by the absorbed couple on the settee, but nervertheless Jonas swung her slightly away from them as his mouth curled in a brief smile, his teeth white against his tanned skin as he murmured, 'I don't mind in the least, but I rather think those two over there might.'

Puzzled, Sara glanced over to where Vanessa and Sam were sitting.

'If your brother wants to be alone with my sister, he can hardly invite her to walk round the garden with him, can he?'

Sara felt her skin colour up hotly beneath the implied criticism that she was lacking in tact and intuition. For a moment it struck her that if Sam were genuinely interested in Vanessa and a permanent relationship developed from that interest, her own life would change dramatically. If Sam married again, she could hardly go on living with him.

Engrossed in her painful thoughts, she was manoeuvred through the door and out on to the patio before she realised what was happening.

As she tugged her arm away from his grip, her toes, exposed by her flimsy sandals, were caught painfully by the flaking edge of one of the bricks. She lost her balance slightly and would have stumbled if Jonas hadn't caught her.

The moment his arms went round her she froze. It was happening again. The moment he touched her she could feel the rivulets of fire building up inside her.

'I don't know what it is about you,' he teased against her ear, 'but every time I get you in my arms . . .'

'Let go of me . . .' Her voice was husky and impassioned, her mind revolting against the thought that her body dared to feel such inappropriate desire.

'How long has it been since the accident?'

The question caught her off guard, and she had replied before she could stop herself.

'Eighteen months?' Jonas released her, standing back a little from her so that he could look into her face. 'And you're still mourning him, aren't you?'

His voice was unexpectedly gentle, filling her with a need to lash out at him. She didn't want his sympathy.

'I'll always mourn him,' she told him bitingly.

She heard him sigh, his face tightening slightly. He stepped back from her and crouched down on the patio, examining the flaking bricks.

'This will have to come up before the winter, otherwise it will deteriorate even further.'

'Come up?' Sara was shocked. 'No . . . I want it to stay. It's lovely.'

'It's crumbling away and it's dangerous. What would have happened if that had been Sam who stumbled just then?'

The logical force of his argument couldn't be denied.

'Nothing lasts for ever,' he told her curtly, and Sara had the impression he wasn't merely talking about the bricks. If he was trying to tell her that she couldn't spend the rest of her life mourning for Rick, he was wrong. She could, and she fully intended to do so.

A sharp tap on the window startled her and she turned round to discover Vanessa beckoning them inside.

'I think we've trespassed on your hospitality long enough for one evening,' she said warmly to Sara as she and Jonas walked back in. 'I can't tell you how much I enjoyed the meal. All three of you must come and eat with us next time, although I can't promise anything very exciting.'

It struck Sara quite forcibly that her discussion with Sam had totally eased away nearly all of Vanessa's earlier uncertainty, and she looked thoughtfully across at her brother, who was smiling affectionately at their blonde visitor.

A sound from upstairs made Sara frown. 'That's Carly,' she pronounced. 'She isn't completely used to her new surroundings yet, and she tends to wake up during the night. I'll go up and check on her.'

'I'd like to come with you, if I may. That's if a strange face won't frighten her?'

'When it's as pretty as yours?' Sam teased. 'Well, I certainly wouldn't be frightened by waking up to it.'

The words held a subtle sexuality that made Vanessa's fair skin flush. Automatically Sara glanced across the room to Jonas, who responded to her by lifting his eyebrows, his mouth curling slightly as though to say, 'I told you so.'

'No . . . come on up.'

Carly was sitting up in bed rubbing her eyes, her hair curling untidily round her head. She beamed a delighted smile at Sara as she opened the door, her eyes rounding slightly as she saw Vanessa.

'My teddy fell off the bed, and I think he's hurt his head,' she announced, speaking to Sara but looking at Vanessa.

Trying to sound severe, Sara teased, 'Fell off? I think you mean a certain little girl kicked him off in her sleep don't you?'

Carly giggled and smiled at Vanessa.

'You've got very pretty hair,' she told her frankly. 'It's the same colour as my mummy's was, isn't it, Sara?'

Sara was never quite sure how much Carly remembered of her life before the accident, but she and Sam made it a rule to allow her to talk as freely about her mother as she wished, without encouraging her to do so in any way that was morbid.

'Very similar,' she said honestly now, 'although Vanessa's is more silvery than your mummy's.'

'It looks like angel hair. I wish mine was that colour.'

'She's learning early,' Sara laughed, ruffling her niece's curly locks.

'Would you like to read me a story?'

The invitation, offered to Vanessa very much with the air of royalty bestowing a favour on a humble suitor, made Sara smile, but she still said firmly, 'Vanessa is just going home, and she's too tired to read to you now.' She saw Carly's face start to crumple and offered palliatively, 'She has invited us to go to her house tomorrow though. She's been looking after the cats and dog for us.'

Once again the childish eyes rounded. Vanessa, who had been clutching the retrieved teddy, leaned over the bed and tucked it in alongside Carly.

As she straightened up, Carly leaned forwards and gave her a noisy kiss. She was always an affectionate child; Sara had encouraged her to be demonstrative. She and Sam had been brought up by parents who loved them very much but who were physically rather remote, and they had both agreed that they didn't want that for Carly. Watching the delighted pleasure in Vanessa's eyes as she willingly complied with Carly's request to be tucked in by her, Sara was glad that the little girl had taken to her, and yet at the same time she was conscious of feeling very much alone, aware that she and Sam were no longer attuned to one another in the way that they had been following the accident.

On her way downstairs, Vanessa made firm arrangements for the following afternoon. Jonas was waiting in the hall for his sister, and they left almost immediately.

'Nice couple, aren't they?' commented Sam as he helped her to wash the coffee cups, adding teasingly, 'Not a bit in the Wayne Houseley mould at all, is he?'

'I like Vanessa, but he isn't my type,' Sara said shortly, feeling the need to expand on her statement when Sam raised his eyebrows a little and frowned. 'He's too sure of himself, Sam . . . Too . . .'

'Male?' he supplied rather drily, shocking her with his percipience. He put down the cloth he was using to dry the cups and came over to her, taking hold of her hands in his and turning them over. For several seconds he seemed lost in contemplation of her palms, but when he lifted his head his expression was extremely grave.

'Perhaps now isn't the time to say so, Sara, but I'm worried about you. Life dealt you a terrible blow when Rick was killed—I know that—but you can't mourn him for ever, my love. You must learn to love and let go. You're hanging on to your grief . . . fostering it almost. You've become almost compulsive about it . . . turned in on yourself too much. You've built your life round Carly and me, and that's not right . . . not for a girl of your age. You should get out more.'

'Find someone else?' Sara's voice was brittle. Snatching her hands away from him, she turned her back and demanded in a harsh voice. 'Is that what you're planning on doing, Sam? Finding someone else to take Holly's place . . . or have you already found her?'

Tears pricked her eyes as she threw down her cloth and fled to her room. What was the matter with her? she asked herself as she curled up in the chair in front of her window. She had just quarrelled bitterly with her brother, something that had never happened before, and why? Because she was fighting like a cornered creature, terrified of the way she could feel her life changing around her, and illogically she blamed those changes on Jonas.

Downstairs she had said things to Sam that she had no right to say—and had thought worse. She had deliberately tried to make him feel guilty, to insinuate that he had no right to love someone else, that he was betraying Holly in doing so. And that was wrong.

Uncurling herself from her chair, she went tiredly downstairs and knocked on Sam's door.

When he opened it she saw the unhappiness in his eyes, and went straight into his arms.

'Sam, I'm so sorry,' she choked into his shoulder. 'I don't know what got into me; please forgive me.'

'You didn't say anything to me that I haven't said to myself since I met Vanessa,' he told her quietly, making no pretence of not understanding. 'I know what you're thinking, Sara. I've thought it myself, but it's taken meeting Vanessa for me to realise what you and I were doing. We've lost two people we love very dearly—nothing can change that—but neither of them would want us to spend the rest of our lives refusing to accept and share love with someone else because of that. In their place, would you? Would you honestly want Rick to spend his life alone grieving for you if the positions had been reversed?'

Would she? Perhaps not, but that didn't change how she felt. Unlike Sam, she didn't *want* to love anyone else. Love meant pain, uncertainty.

'It's serious between you and Vanessa, then?' she asked him without answering.

'It could be. I haven't known her long, after all. I've only met her four times before tonight. She showed me round the cottage the first time then I came down.'

'And she was the one you fell in love with, not the cottage as you told me,' Sara tried to tease.

'I should have talked to you about her before, but it was all so sudden, and she's so shy and insecure that I don't want to rush her.' He made a wry face. 'After all, even if something does develop between us, she won't be getting any bargain, will she?' He glanced at his wheelchair and said quietly, 'I know I'm making good progress, but I'll probably never be entirely free of that . . .'

'If she loves you that won't make any difference,' Sara assured him swiftly.

'Ah yes . . . *if* she loves me . . .'

'You didn't tell me that she and her brother were looking after Miss Betts's animals, or about Miss Betts's relationship with their uncle.'

'Mmm? No, I didn't, did I?' There was a faintly ironical gleam in his eyes. 'You seemed so dead set against Jonas it seemed a shame to tell you the truth. It was the first spark of emotion I'd seen in you since the funeral. You're taking Carly round tomorrow when you go to collect the animals, then?'

'Yes . . . if you don't mind?'

'Of course not.' He stretched and winced slightly.

'That reminds me, I've got a hospital appointment pending. I'd better check when it is.' Since his discharge from hospital, Sam had to go for regular physiotherapy sessions, and these had now been transferred from the London hospital he had previously attended to a more local one. 'Vanessa offered to run me there and back any time you were otherwise occupied, by the way.' He grinned slightly shamefacedly at her. 'I told her it could be quite awkward for you, now that you've got Carly at home from school. She's bound to get bored hanging around the hospital waiting for me.'

It was unreasonable of her to feel this jealously and slight resentment against Sam, Sara told herself later as she prepared for bed. That it sprang from fear she already knew; she liked Vanessa and in other circumstances would have been pleased about the relationship developing between them, but now she felt betrayed and very much alone.

As always when she closed her eyes she conjured up Rick's image, or at least she tried to do. Disturbingly, on this occasion his beloved features refused to form, and instead all she could see was Jonas's arrogantly handsome face and mocking grey eyes.

She always looked forward to this part of the day, this secret communion with Rick when she allowed herself the pleasure of denying to herself that he was dead, but now it seemed that even that had been taken from her.

Cursing Jonas, she turned her face into her pillow and prayed for sleep.

'Well, what sort of dog is it?'

'I'm not sure,' Sara told her niece as they walked hand in hand down the gravel drive that led to their neighbour's house.

Following Vanessa's instructions, she had driven along the main road, until she got to the impressive wrought-iron gates that marked the entrance to the house. They had been left open, the gravel drive curving away through massed rhododendron bushes and specimen trees set in immaculate lawns, and opening out at the front of the house. Sara had parked her car next to a pale green estate car which she guessed must belong to Vanessa.

From the front the house looked every bit as impressive as she had been told, although perhaps impressive wasn't the right word, for it conveyed a cold hauteur the house did not possess. Rather it presented a warm, welcoming façade to the visitor, suggestive of a house that had known the happiness and warmth of many generations of busy family life.

The red brick was softened with age, ivy clinging to the walls. Elegantly proportioned white-painted sash windows looked out over the drive and grounds.

As she turned her head, Sara caught the glimmer of sunlight on water.

The door opened as she stood absorbing the scenery, and Vanessa came running down the steps to welcome them.

'Right on time,' she greeted them, pushing down the enthusiastic Old English sheepdog puppy who had jumped up at Sara. 'Jonas's dog,' she told Sara with a smile. 'Mum bought him for Jonas for his birthday to replace the old dog he lost last year.'

'Where's our dog?' Carly asked Vanessa importantly, reaching down to pat the puppy's curly head.

'He's in the kitchen at the moment. Why don't you come in and say hello to him?'

Nodding eagerly, Carly let Vanessa take her hand and guide her up the steps.

'I had planned for us to have tea first,' Vanessa apologised to Sara as they headed straight for the kitchen, 'but something tells me that Carly wouldn't think that a good idea.'

As they walked through it, Sara noted the lovely proportions of the hallway, with its airy wrought-iron staircase and marble steps. Several portraits graced the walls, family ones, Sara suspected; her suspicions were confirmed when Vanessa commented, opening a thick, richly polished mahogany door, 'The house has been in Jonas's family for a long time, but gradually over the years the family has had to sell off more and more land, so all that's left now is the house and its grounds. That's why Jonas wanted to buy the paddock off Miss Betts. He could use it to expand the business. The cottage was once part of the estate, and it was sold to Miss Betts's parents by Jonas's great-grandfather.'

Vanessa stopped to let Carly and Sara precede her into the kitchen. A solid-looking Aga filled a brick alcove and the kitchen units had wooden doors, the wood looking heavy and old. A large refectory-style table filled the centre of the floor.

'Unless we're entertaining, we normally eat in here,' said Vanessa. 'Jonas needs a proper meal at lunchtime, but he never has time to sit down and eat properly, never mind getting changed, so we tend to eat here in the kitchen. Fortunately he's having a bit of a lull at the moment. Obviously our season runs ahead of the retailers, and we should have a pretty quiet time from now until late summer when we have to start making up the orders for autumn planting. Mind you, with so much container-grown stuff these days, Jonas is always kept busy. It's a very competitive and demanding business, and if we can't satisfy a customer's requirements, they'll pretty soon go somewhere else.

'Jonas should be in in about an hour,' she added. 'He normally has something to eat about five, and then goes out again to do some more work. We have to take advantage of the light evenings while we can. I'll get him to show you round if you like. Sam said you were very keen to get to grips with the garden at the cottage.'

Fortunately, before Sara was forced to reply, Carly spotted the golden retriever basking in front of the Aga.

'Is that our dog?' she asked Vanessa eagerly.

'Yes, that's Simon,' confirmed Vanessa, reaching up to push the tumbled curls off Carly's excited face. If Carly had to have a stepmother she'd be hard put to find one who could love her more then Vanessa, Sara reflected, watching the emotion play over the other woman's face.

'She's so lovely,' Vanessa said huskily as Carly ran off and crouched down beside the dog, patting the golden head and crooning nonsense in the fluffy ear. 'The cats are in the conservatory,' she added. 'We have a small goldfish pond in there, and they're living under the illusion that one day they're going to catch their own tea.'

Watching her ten minutes later as she took a glass of

orange juice to Carly, Sara was again struck by the intensity of emotion the little girl seemed to arouse in Vanessa.

'You obviously love children very much,' she commented when Vanessa came back to pour their tea.

The blue eyes became shadowed, her mouth trembling slightly. 'Yes ... I do,' she agreed huskily. She seemed as though she was about to burst into tears, and Sara felt slightly uncomfortable. Had she said something to upset Vanessa? She had already realised how sensitive the other woman was, and she hated to think she had hurt her, however inadvertently.

'I'm sorry about this,' Vanessa managed. 'I'm not normally so ... so emotional. It's just that ... Well, I may as well tell you. When I was eighteen I was pregnant. I wasn't married. My ... my lover was, though. He was someone I'd met through school— older than me. I behaved stupidly, but at eighteen ...' She shrugged. 'You know how it is, you think you know it all. Of course I'd kept the relationship secret from the parents. Jonas was working in Canada at the time, and when I told him about the baby my lover insisted that I had to have an abortion. I didn't want to ... but I was too scared to confide in my mother. I had no close friends to talk to. It was already arranged that I would go to Cambridge if my A-level grades were good enough. I allowed him to persuade me. Unfortunately something went wrong, and I was very ill.'

Her eyes avoided Sara's, but it didn't take much imagination to sense how desperately unhappy she must have been. Sara felt bitterly appalled that any responsible adult could inveigle an adolescent into such a damaging situation. No doubt her lover had been anxious for Vanessa to have an abortion, especially since he was married, no doubt with children by his wife. She felt towards him as she had done towards Wayne Houseley, only in this instance her sick disgust and revulsion was, if anything, even stronger.

'The parents had to be told, of course. They were marvellous—so supportive and understanding. Jonas came home on holiday and when he found out what had happened . . .' She shuddered. 'He wanted to confront my lover with what he had done, but his father managed to dissuade him by pointing out to him that innocent people would also have to suffer— his wife and two sons. I've wished so many times since then that I'd had my child. Sometimes I can't forgive myself for giving in so weakly. The man concerned means nothing to me now, but a child . . .'

Sara thought she understood, now, the reason for Vanessa's shyness and insecurity. It must be incredibly damaging to have your child and your love rejected by your lover.

'I've told Sam about it . . .'

Deep in thought, Sara took several seconds to register Vanessa's comment. When she did she said softly, 'I'm sure he understood how you must have felt, Vanessa.'

Sara knew her brother well enough to know he would be the last person to condemn any woman for something so completely beyond her control.

'Yes . . . Yes, he did. I really like him, Sara,' she

added shyly. 'And Carly . . . I've always wanted a little girl.'

Sensing that Vanessa was trying to gauge whether her relationship with Sam was going to elicit her disapproval, Sara told her firmly, 'And he really likes you. I'm glad he's found someone to . . . to help him to build a new life, Vanessa. It's what he needs and it's what Holly would have wanted for him.'

It was only as she said the words that Sara realised how true they were. Holly wouldn't have wanted her husband and daughter to spend the rest of their lives in mourning for her. Just as Rick wouldn't have wanted her . . . Frantically she tried to dismiss her thoughts. She wanted to go on mourning Rick. She needed . . . Needed?

She was glad of the diversion created by Carly, who came up to ask when she could see the cats.

Lifting the little girl on to her knee, she promised her that they would go and see them just as soon as she had drunk her tea.

CHAPTER FIVE

IT was only when she came to leave that Sara realised the impossibility of bundling one extremely large dog, plus two cats and a small child, into her very small car. Gazing helplessly at Simon's bulk and Carly's mutinous face at her suggestion that they leave the dog behind until another day, she was relieved when Vanessa came to her rescue.

'Look, why don't I run Simon, the cats and Carly back in my estate car?' she suggested.

A faint tinge of colour warmed her skin, and Sara guessed sympathetically that she would be glad of the excuse to see Sam again. 'Fine,' she thanked her. 'I'll follow you in my car.'

Vanessa bit her lip. 'Oh, I'd forgotten—I've got an important message to give Jonas. One of his buyers wants to come and see him tomorrow morning at ten, and I think he had planned to be out. Sara, would you mind staying behind until he comes in? He won't be long, only about half an hour. It would be a good opportunity for him to show you round the greenhouses as well.'

Sara wanted to refuse, but Vanessa was so sensitive to the least nuance of criticism that if she did so, she might think that Sara didn't trust her to take care of Carly, or, worse still, that she disapproved of her relationship with Sam.

'OK, I'll stay and give Jonas his message,' she

agreed, adding with a faint grimace in Carly's direction, 'you might tell Sam, though, that a certain young lady ought to have a bath and an early bedtime tonight.'

'I'll tell him,' Vanessa promised, ushering her charges into her car. Sara was pleased to see that she put Carly in the back, carefully fastening the seat belt around her. At her side, Simon perched regally on the seat, the two cats in their baskets in the back.

As she drove past her, Vanessa rolled down her window, and called cheerfully, 'Thanks, Sara; Jonas shouldn't be long.'

He wasn't. She had been waiting in the kitchen for less than fifteen minutes when she heard the Land Rover draw up outside.

As he strode into the kitchen, he checked, eyebrows lifting in mute query as he saw her.

'I couldn't get Simon and the cats and Carly into my car, so Vanessa has run them back,' she told him curtly. 'Vanessa asked me to stay behind to give you a message.'

'Can it wait until I've had a shower?' he asked, grimacing faintly. 'I'm filthy.'

He didn't look it, but as he turned round she saw the patches of sweat down the back of his shirt, and she saw there were smears of mud on his arms, below his rolled up sleeves.

'I've spent most of the afternoon digging out what we hope is going to be a breeding pond for koi carp. It's a side-line I'm thinking of going into in a small way.' He flexed his back and grimaced again. 'God, I'm going to stiff tomorrow!'

He tensed his torso exploratively and then relaxed it. Sara had been watching him out of the corner of her eye, and she felt the alien heat prickle over her skin, her muscles locking against the treacherous sensation.

Jonas was watching her, his eyes narrowing in mocking comprehension as he drawled flippantly, 'I don't suppose there's any point in inviting you to come up and scrub my back, is there?'

'None at all,' Sara replied crisply, resenting both the lazy amusement in his eyes and her own colourful blush.

'Give me ten minutes and I'll be down,' was Jonas's parting comment as he headed for the hall, throwing over his shoulder as he opened the door, 'oh, and I wouldn't mind a cup of coffee if there's any going?'

Telling herself that it was only because she had nothing else to do that she was complying with his request, Sara set about making some fresh coffee.

True to his word, Jonas was back downstairs within ten minutes almost to the second. He came into the kitchen, bringing with him a clean smell of soap. His hair clung damply to his scalp, his bare forearms and exposed throat gleaming like polished satin.

Deliberately keeping the width of the table between them, Sara poured his coffee and gave him his message.

'I'll get back now,' she concluded curtly, trying not to notice the clean neatness of his hands and nails, only the odd rough callous and his strong tan betraying the fact that he worked outdoors.

'Why the rush?' His tone was laconic. 'Sam will be perfectly safe with Vanessa, or is that why you're so keen to get back? Or don't you approve?'

She didn't pretend not to understand, her skin flushing with angry colour as she vehemently denied his suggestion.

'So it doesn't worry you that a . . . relationship could well develop between my sister and your brother?'

'Not at all; why should it?'

'No reason, but I must admit to being rather surprised. You're so determined to keep on living in the past yourself that I thought you could well resent Sam's decision to go on living.'

It was a cruel thing to say, but there was no regret or apology in the grey eyes as they locked on hers. In fact, he seemed to be regarding her with a fierce banked-down anger that made her pulses jolt and her defence system spring to the alert.

'Why is it you're so eager to put me in the wrong?'

It was a silly question to have asked, and when she saw the derisory glint in his eyes, Sara wished it unsaid.

'Perhaps because it stops me from being equally eager to do this . . .' He put down his coffee mug and moved so quickly that there wasn't time to avoid him.

The hard pressure of his body against hers forced her back against the table until she could feel the edge of it against her back.

She raised her hands to his chest to push him away, but it was like trying to move solid rock, as he slowly made her arch backwards. The hands she had raised to fend him off locked round his neck to stop her from overbalancing completely. As though he sensed how much her mind was fighting against him, despite the fact that he had subdued her body, the pressure of his mouth on hers betrayed anger as well as desire.

She didn't want to respond to him, but the fierce heat of his kiss aroused a treacherous response inside her. His teeth tugged urgently at her bottom lip, his tongue taking full advantage of her sharp cry of protest, the smothered sound of satisfaction he made against her mouth dangerously erotic.

She disliked him; she hated him almost and loathed the physical effect he had on her, but none of those things could obliterate the fact that he aroused her. In his arms she experienced a need and responsiveness she had not even felt with Rick.

Her fingernails curled into his back as she fought the treacherous thought, wanting to deny it, but knowing it was too late. Irrationally, the knowledge that he could arouse her made her resent him even more. Her feelings towards him seemed to mirror those of Eve towards the serpent who tempted her and was thus instrumental in destroying her innocent paradise.

Jonas groaned as her nails raked against his shirt-clad back, and it gave her a savage sense of satisfaction to think that she had hurt him, until she saw the hectic flush of colour staining his skin and felt his body's immediate arousal. His hands held her hips, imprisoning her against the swollen pressure of his thighs.

Rick had never touched her like this, had never blatantly imposed his sexuality upon her in the way that Jonas was doing. His behaviour towards her had always been gentle and restrained, his kisses tender rather than demanding.

Sara drank in air greedily as Jonas released her mouth, her breasts rising and falling hurriedly. The darkness in Jonas's eyes as his hands moved up over her back, pressing the rounded warmth of her breasts into his chest, almost strangled her breath in her lungs. The harsh, almost tormented sound he made in his throat was shockingly painful. She found herself caught in wholly unexpected and very dangerous cross-currents, her body telling her one thing while her mind screamed another, and then miraculously Jonas was releasing her, freeing her from the dark spell of his physical dominance.

'Have dinner with me tonight?'

His voice was slurred, dark coins of colour still staining the high cheekbones, his eyes almost black with arousal.

Automatically she eased herself away from him, gasping at the pain stabbing through her back.

'No ...'

She saw his mouth tighten and could almost sense his frustration.

'If you won't come for my sake, then how about making the sacrifice for your brother's?' he suggested tightly.

'Sam?'

The expression of hostility and bitterness in his eyes would have frightened her if she hadn't been so angry with him.

'Is it so unbelievable that he might want Vanessa to himself? Think about it; the way he is at the moment he can hardly invite her out. They haven't had much opportunity to be alone together. You guard him like a mother hen with one chick.'

His use of the word 'guard' and the sardonic expression in his eyes galled her. Her mouth compress-

ing, Sara was just about to refuse for a second time
when she remembered what Sam had said to her about
Vanessa. Jonas was right, Sam *would* welcome an
opportunity to have Vanessa to himself, and it was
hardly fair of her to deny it to him simply because
Jonas had been the one to point it out to her.

'I can't go out to dinner dressed like this!' she
pointed out to him.

He shrugged powerful shoulders. 'So you need to go
home and get changed. I'll pick you up in an hour.'

She didn't want to go out to dinner with him, but it
suddenly struck her that he was giving her the ideal
opportunity to tell him how little she welcomed his
advances. At least in the civilisation of a restaurant,
surrounded by other people, she would safely be able
to tell him that she wanted him to leave her alone.

'All right.'

She watched as he grimaced, his voice rough as he
told her, 'Don't overtax yourself in showing enthusiasm, will you? And don't try backing out,' he added
softly as he walked with her to her car. 'Because I'm
perfectly capable of making sure you go through with
it.'

Sara didn't doubt it.

Vanessa showed a remarkable lack of suprise when
she announced that she was dining with Jonas, and it
struck her that perhaps the whole thing had been
arranged between brother and sister beforehand. It
seemed unlike Vanessa to involve herself in anything
in the slightest way underhand, but if she was in love
with Sam, wasn't it only natural that she should want
to snatch at any opportunity to be alone with him?
Strangely, the fact that Jonas might genuinely be

taking her out merely to facilitate his sister's relationship with her brother was not the relief it should have
been.

To punish herself for her weakness, she deliberately
changed into the dress she had bought for Rick's
annual office 'do'. It had never been worn because
Rick had been killed before the dinner dance took
place, and now, as she removed it from its protective
wrapping, Sara shuddered slightly, suddenly realising
that for the first time, when she thought about Rick,
his mental image had not automatically formed in her
mind. In fact, when she tried to conjure up his familiar
features they stubbornly refused to appear, and she
rushed in panic to her dressing table to snatch up his
photograph.

The sight of his familiar smile eased her tension.
Holding the photograph in front of her, she felt her
breathing ease and her heartbeat slow down.

Knowing that if she wasn't ready on time Jonas was
perfectly capable of coming upstairs to discover why,
she showered and changed in almost record time. She
was just putting the final touches to her make-up when
she heard a car outside.

'Jonas is here,' Vanessa called up to her.

'I'm coming down now.'

Pulling a brush through her hair, she snatched up
her bag and hurried to the door. A glimpse of herself in
her full-length mirror threw back a reflection that was
startingly unfamiliar. It had been so long since she had
even thought of dressing up that the sight of herself
made her check and stare.

She had always been a slim girl, but not all of the

weight she had lost in the first few weeks after the accident had been regained, and the dress, which had fitted snugly when she had bought it, was now just loose enough to hint at a delicate fragility. The long sleeves ended in tight cuffs which seemed to emphasise the narrowness of her wrist bones. The bodice of the dress was cut high on her throat at the front, dipping very low at the back to expose her skin. The silky-fine fabric hugged her waist, flaring out gently over her hips. The neckline and low back were etched in a deep band of satin, like the wrist bands and at the back of her neck the dress fastened in an ornamental satin bow.

Its misty lilac colour seemed to emphasise the delicacy of her skin, turning her eyes from blue to amethyst, and imparting a deeper lustre to her hair.

It was a dress that a woman bought with a man very much in mind, and that she should be wearing it tonight for Jonas and not Rick, tore at her heart with sharp knives of anguish—all the more intense because she recognised that one treacherous part of her did want to dress for Jonas, no matter how much her heart and mind might resent it.

Vanessa was waiting for her at the bottom of the stairs, her face lighting up in an appreciative expression when she saw her.

'Jonas, just wait until you see this!' she called out gaily to her brother.

A choking panicky feeling closed up Sara's throat as she recognised that Vanessa was openly hinting that Jonas would find her sexually desirable. It was on the tip of her tongue to announce that she had changed her mind, but as Jonas appeared in the doorway to the sitting-room and studied her with a steel-grey glint in his eyes, Sara knew that any attempt on her part to extricate herself from their date would meet with very severe resistance.

It was for Sam's sake that she was doing this, she reminded herself as she allowed Jonas to hand her into his car.

To see a Rolls-Royce outside the door, even if rather an old one, was not what she had expected, and it was Vanessa who, correctly reading her surprise, laughed and said bubblingly, 'It belonged to Jonas's uncle, and it had done such a small mileage and had been so carefully looked after that it seemed a waste to get rid of it. I think it suits him, although Jonas prefers his Land Rover.'

'It does have its advantages,' drawled Jonas, interrupting his sister.

'Yes, it's got seats that recline—unlike the Land Rover,' Vanessa teased, and even though Sara knew her remark had been directed at Jonas rather than herself, she could not help her skin going hot with betraying colour as Jonas helped her into the luxurious car.

As he closed her door, the rich smell of the leather upholstery engulfed her, and she could not resist stroking an appreciative finger along the burr-walnut panelling.

Even with her eyes averted, she was aware of the exact moment Jonas slid into the driver's seat. His door closed with a dull thunk, and he switched on the engine.

There was a moment's delay while he fastened his seat belt, and then, just when she expected him to drive away, he told her coolly, 'You mustn't take Vanessa's remark too much to heart; I promise you I'm way, way past the stage where I attempt to make love to my dates on the front seat of a parked car. These days I prefer the comfort and privacy of a large double bed.'

The images so unexpectedly conjured up by his drawled words were so disturbing that Sara had to take refuge from them by staring fixedly out of her window. If she looked at Jonas now he would see quite plainly that in her mind's eye she had seen that double bed and that, moreover, the slim female body entwined with his on it had quite unmistakably been her own.

The intensity of her arousal frightened her, making gooseflesh shiver over her skin. What was happening to her? She didn't *want* this to happen. She didn't *want* to feel this way about him . . . about any man! She had already lost one man she had loved; she couldn't bear to lose another, and the only way to prevent that from happening was not to let herself fall in love again.

Fall in love? That was impossible. She could never fall in love again; she loved Rick. The familiarity of her thought patterns was reassuringly soothing, and helped her to dismiss the sudden surge of desire Jonas's comments had aroused. Even so, she felt bitterly resentful that he seemed to have this almost frightening ability to bring such a strong surge of sexuality out in her. It made her feel unsure of herself, and dangerously vulnerable, that a man she disliked so strongly as a human being should have such a powerful effect on her physically. It was disturbing to realise that she was not fully in control of her own responses, that part of her could be so wilfully blind to the strictures of her mind.

'That's a very attractive dress you're wearing.' Jonas observed. 'It has a touchable quality that seems to be missing from a good many modern fashions. Almost, dare I say it, a quality of sensuousness that's very appealing to my sex. I'm flattered that you chose to wear it for me.'

His last comment was delivered in a tone so soft and low that Sara barely caught the words. When she did she froze, and turned to glare glacially at him.

'I didn't choose to wear it for you,' she told him bitingly, 'I had to wear it because it happens to be the only evening dress in my wardrobe.'

That wasn't strictly true, but in her intensely emotional state she wasn't prepared to recognise her own lie, her eyes flashing angry warning signs as his attention shifted momentarily from the road to her face.

Sensing that he didn't believe her, she added hotly, 'If you must know, I brought this dress to wear for . . . for my fiancé, only he was killed before . . .'

She broke off, conscious that her throat was so thick with tears that to continue talking would be to subject herself to the indignity of breaking down completely in front of her tormentor.

Without knowing why, she sensed that to be held in Jonas's arms while she sobbed out her misery and guilt against his shoulder would shift the axis of their relationship completely, and that was something she didn't want. She wanted to resent and dislike him, she recognised numbly. She didn't want to admit that he might have characteristics that she could find attractive—and why? Because she was frightened of what that admission might mean.

Engrossed in her own thought, she was conscious of him swearing and the car swerving sharply. As her seat belt reacted to his momentary sharp pressure on the brakes, she felt it bite into her flesh.

At first she thought he had braked to avoid a bird, or perhaps a rabbit, but when she saw the look of bitter fury on his face as he turned towards her, his knuckles almost white as he gripped the steering wheel, Sara realised that she was responsible for their abrupt halt.

As his hands left the steering wheel and gripped her shoulders, her seat belt prevented her from cringing away from him. His eyes had the metallic gleam of someone pushed beyond their limits, the tension whitening the skin round his mouth and nose, making her shiver in sick apprehension.

'If I thought for one momet that you were trying to substitute me for your dead lover, I'd . . .'

'Substitute *you* for Rick?' Sara felt her own anger rise to meet his, only hers was an anger that was spiked with fear: fear of him and fear of herself, combined with a sure knowledge that she was running headlong into the very situation she had been determined to avoid.

She let her anger against herself as well as against him underscore her words with scorn.

'You could never take Rick's place,' she told him heatedly. 'You're not half the man he is. You never could be. You . . . What do you think you're doing?' she demanded thickly as he suddenly re-started the car and turned it round, with impatient jerky movements, driving back to the crossroads at a speed every instinct told her was dangerous.

It struck her as they reached the crossroads that he must be intending to take her home, but instead of turning off, he kept on going until they came to the gates of his house. Only then did he slow down, turning the heavy car into the drive.

'What do you think you're doing?' demanded Sara in panic. 'We're supposed to be going out to dinner . . . to . . .'

'I'm going to do something I should have done the first time I met you,' Jonas told her grimly, bringing the car to a sudden standstill outside the front door. 'I'm going to show you once and for all that your fiancé is dead, and that you and I are very much alive. You can't cling to the past for ever, Sara. It's time you recognised the truth—that your precious Rick is dead . . . that he can never ever again hold you in his arms . . . that no matter how much you might claim you still love him, memories are no substitute for the pleasure of a warm living body in bed beside you . . . a man's hands on your skin, giving you pleasure.'

He caught her wrist as she lifted her open hand to strike him, his grip bruising her fragile bones.

'I'm glad you did that,' he told her thickly, his eyes glittering beneath black narrowed lashes. 'It makes it much easier for me to do this.'

The hard pressure of his lips on hers was shockingly intimate, his tongue thrusting into her mouth in a fierce rhythm that made shivers of erotic sensation slide down her spine.

It must be her anger that was intensifying the

sensation so much, she thought dazedly, fighting against matching his furious assault with her nails and teeth in a response that had nothing to do with making him stop what he was doing to her.

His hands were on her bare back, she realised, his thumbs probing the satin band where it touched the outer curves of her breasts. She shivered as his thumbs eased beneath the fabric, touching her bare skin, and then, shockingly, his hands weren't on her back any more, but were pressing against the chiffon-covered fullness of her breasts.

What was it about this man that so completely destroyed her self-control? she wondered hazily as she felt her nipples peak and thrust tautly against the heat of his palms. The way his fingers tightened on the outer swell of her breasts, his palms pressing against the diamond-hard nipples, told her that he was as aware of her arousal as she was herself. The knowledge should have been humiliating, but, shockingly, it was not.

Indeed, it was almost as though her anger had sparked off a chain of reaction that was leading to some sort of osmosis that completely changed her feelings for him, from dislike to desire.

Lost in the sensations evoked by his mouth and hands, she felt it a shock to be abruptly released. His fingers curled sharply into her arms as he held her at arm's length.

As she tensed against the derisory comment she expected him to make, it was doubly shocking to her to hear him saying thickly, 'I don't know what it is about you that makes me feel like this, Sara; I only know that you're the only woman I've ever met who

arouses me to such a frenzy.' He leaned forward and
touched her half-parted mouth with fingers that
visibly trembled.

'We have to talk,' he told her, 'but not out here.
Let's go inside.'

As though she had suddenly lost the ability to move
independently of him, she let him guide her out of the
car and into the darkened house. Without taking his
hand from her arm, he switched on the hall lights and
then opened the door into what appeared to be a
library-cum-study.

Still shocked by the raw emotion she had heard in
his voice, Sara let him lead her across to a large leather
chesterfield, obediently sinking down on to it, and
watching with wide, bewildered eyes as he sat down
beside her.

His movements were edged with a tension that in a
less aggressive and assured man she might have
thought nervousness, but the thought of any woman
making Jonas nervous, least of all her, was so
ridiculous that she instantly dismissed it.

Now that she was out of his arms and removed from
the powerful spell he seemed to throw over her senses,
she felt a renewal of her earlier hostility and
resentment. The passion that had flared between them
in the car was something she preferred to dismiss.

'I almost wanted to kill you when you told me you
bought that dress for him, do you know that?'

The words were delivered so flatly, it took her
several seconds to realise it was not a joke.

Hard, flat patches of colour burned his cheekbones,
his mouth compressed so tightly that she could see the
fierce beat of the pulse in his throat.

'I want you, Sara,' he continued in the same flat, hard tone. 'I wanted you from the first moment I saw you, but more than that, I'm falling in love with you.'

It took several seconds for his words to sink in. When they had, Sara could only stare at him in incredulous disbelief. He had fallen in love with *her*? Impossible! She opened her mouth to tell him so, and was surprised by the ferocity of the anger and fear that suddenly engulfed her. How dared he claim to love her? Rick had loved her and she had loved him, but Rick had never treated her the way Jonas did. Rick had revered and respected her . . . had never touched her in furious desire and anger. Rick had . . . Rick . . . A sob of pure anguish lodged in her throat, a sense of fear and betrayal flooding her senses. How dared this man claim to love her; how dared he try to seduce her away from her precious memories? She didn't want his love. She didn't want *anyone's* love. Unadmitted, buried deep in her subconscious, was the knowledge that to open oneself to love was to open oneself to pain. She had travelled down that road once in her life; she wasn't going to travel down it again.

With a bitterness that was directed as much against herself as it was against him, she stared at him in incredulity and said, 'Are you actually trying to tell me you think you've fallen in love with me on the strength of a couple of meetings?'

If she hadn't been so angry she might have been amazed at the way he flushed so darkly.

'Improbable, I know.' His voice was harsh and faintly self-derisory, his grimace wry. 'But true none the less. I'm not an impressionable boy, Sara; I admit that falling in love with you wasn't exactly something I anticipated—if I gave it any thought at all I'd begun to assume that it was simply something that wasn't going to happen to me. And to be honest, I didn't regret it. I've seen too much of what 'love' can do to relish the thought of it in my own life, but fate, it seems, had other ideas. The feelings I have for you aren't easy to explain or define, but I know myself well enough to know that they are genuine.' He leaned forward and cupped her chin before she could move out of the way, holding her so that she was forced to meet his eyes.

'And you feel something for me, too,' he finished softly.

Fear kicked painfully in her stomach. 'I don't. I don't feel anything for you,' she lied frantically, trying to pull free of him, but his hand slid round to the back of her neck, holding her immobile.

'I love Rick . . .' she protested. 'I always have and I always will.'

'You love a dead man,' said Jonas bitingly, 'A memory, Sara, a man who can't hold you in his arms any more . . . can't make your body tremble with wanting . . .'

'Stop it! Stop it; I don't want to hear any more!'

'Why?' he demanded fiercely. 'Because it's true? You're clinging to your dead lover because you're afraid to let yourself feel any emotion. You don't love him, not the way I define love. You're clinging to a safe image, because you're too afraid to face the real world.'

'No . . . no . . . you're wrong.' She almost sobbed the words, her throat tight with panic and pain.

'No? Then what's your explanation for this . . . this feeling there is between us—and don't bother trying to deny that there is something . . .?'

She felt herself flush beneath the burning glitter of his eyes, not cold but hot, and bitterly angry.

'Sex,' she told him defensively through a raw throat; 'it's just sex.'

She knew instantly she had made a bad mistake. A smile twisted his mouth, the glitter in his eyes intensifying as he bent his head towards her, his fingers sliding into her hair to cup and caress her head, his mouth moving silkily over hers, generating a heat which forced her to suppress a moan of arousal in her throat.

His hand left her arm and slid to her breast, the intensity of her physical response to him shocking and shaming to her.

It seemed an aeon of time before he let her go, his lips lingering on the swollen contours of hers, caressing and tasting her with a slow and deliberate languor that she found nearly as dangerously overwhelming as his earlier ardour.

For the first time in her life she was aware of the intensity of a man's desire and the urgency of his arousal. Just one word, just a look, in fact, would be enough to take her from his study to the intimacy of the bed he had mentioned to her earlier, and, shamingly, there was still a small part of her that wantonly ached for that intimacy, that yearned to know the satin smoothness of his naked skin, the erotic play of his hands on her body, his mouth . . . She shuddered violently and opened her eyes to see the hot glitter of triumph in his.

'So it's just sex, is it?'

She had to destroy that masculine triumph, to hurt

him the way he was hurting her by trying to make her forget Rick.

'Yes,' she told him fiercely, 'that's all it is.' Recklessly she threw back her head and stared into his eyes. 'I'll go to bed with you, if that's what you want, Jonas, but I don't love you.'

For a moment she held her breath, stupefied by her own recklessness. She watched as his eyes hardened, his mouth compressing with open cruelty.

'So you'll go to bed with me, will you? Why? So that you can relieve the frustration of loving a dead man? Oh no, Sara,' he told her with soft venom. 'There's no way I'm playing that game. Sorry to disappoint you,' he added, subjecting her to an insultingly sexual inspection that told her he was both aware of and unmoved by her arousal. 'I'm afraid you're just going to have to burn,' he taunted her. 'I'll take you home now,' he added coolly. 'Think of me tonight when you're all alone in your cold little bed.'

Sara's emotions were too close to the surface to allow any degree of self-control. Shaking with a mixture of longing and hatred, she said thickly, 'My bed isn't cold, and I won't be alone, Jonas. Rick lives on in my mind and my heart, even if he isn't with me in the flesh.'

For a moment she thought he might actually strike her. She could see his muscles tense under his savage attempt at self-control, and as he threw open the door and strode out into the hall without a word to her, she almost wished he *had* hit her. On a wave of sickening self-knowledge, she recognised that part of her had actually, even if it was only for a second, wanted his physical abuse of her, because in hitting her, in giving way to the emotions she had deliberately aroused in him, he would have given her a genuine reason to resent and despise him. As it was, as he drove her home in an icy cold silence, the person she despised was herself.

Luckily Vanessa and Sam were too engrossed in one another to express anything more than concern at her excuse that she had returned early because of a headache. It was only when Sara was alone in bed that she was able to examine in more detail the improbability of Jonas actually being in love with her, and the intensity of her own fear that he should be. Fear sprang from an inner admission of one's own vulnerability; she knew that. She shivered. If she was vulnerable to Jonas, it was only sexually. Sexually he could arouse her, but that didn't mean she loved him or wanted his love. She didn't.

It seemed incredible that she could have aroused such deep feelings in him in such a short space of time. She and Rick had fallen in love slowly and gradually, gently almost. And yet she knew Jonas hadn't been lying to her. The truth had been there in his eyes, his feelings laid bare for her to read. For the first time it struck her how hard it must have been for a man of his stamp to openly admit his feelings for her. Or had it simply never struck him that they might not be reciprocated? It would be typical of his arrogance, Sara told herself, finding release for her guilt in the thought.

CHAPTER SIX

FOR three days they saw nothing of either Jonas or Vanessa, and Sara told herself that she was glad that Jonas had decided to accept the fact that she just wasn't interested in him.

A spell of thundery weather kept her out of the garden, but there was still plenty to do inside the house. However, Sara was not so sure now that she should be the one to choose its new décor, and when she was alone with Sam one afternoon, she decided to raise the subject with him.

'We haven't seen much of Vanessa lately,' she commented, and watched him scowl.

'I told her to stay away.' He looked up in time to catch the shock in Sara's eyes, and moved restlessly in his chair. 'It's no use, Sara,' he told her. 'What can I possibly offer a woman? My legs will never be as they were; I'm going to have to spend a considerable amount of my life in this chair; I've got a six-year-old daughter and all the emotional baggage that comes from having a committed relationship. If Vanessa was less sensitive, less easily hurt . . .'

'She wouldn't be the woman you love,' Sara said quietly. 'And you do love her, don't you, Sam?'

'Too much to tie her down to the sort of life she'd have with me. Financially I'm comfortably off, I know, but I can't offer her anything that compares with what Jonas gives her.'

'No, but you can give her something she wants far more. She loves you,' Sara told him. 'If I wasn't sure that you loved her I'd agree with what you're doing, but you do love her. And if it's me you're worrying about, then don't,' she added crisply. 'I can soon bring my secretarial training up to date and get a job . . .'

'You'll always have a home with me, Sara,' Sam interrupted roughly. 'And Vanessa knows that. If I could be sure that she wasn't acting out of some misguided sense of pity . . .' he burst out emotionally, his face muscles tense and compressed. 'She offered to drive me in to Dorchester for my hospital check up tomorrow, but I told her you'd take me . . .'

Hesitating only for a moment, Sara said coolly, 'Then you'd better telephone her and tell her that you've changed your mind, because I can't. I've got a date of my own that I can't break, tomorrow afternoon.'

'With Jonas?' her brother grinned teasingly at her. 'Aha, I thought you weren't as immune as you've been claiming! Vanessa will be over the moon; she's convinced that you're the ideal girl for him. She says she's never seen him get in such a state over any woman before.'

She had made up her fictitious date on the spur of the moment, determined to give Vanessa an opportunity to convince Sam that her feelings were genuine, but she was appalled that Sam should leap to the conclusion that her supposed date must be with Jonas.

However, her brother was frowning again, his movements as he levered himself out of his chair and walked haltingly over to the French windows, jerky with tension and frustration. 'I can't just ring her up like that and tell her I've changed my mind,' he protested. 'Besides,' he added roughly, 'whatever she may or may not feel for me, everything I've already said holds good. She might think she cares for me now, but she knows nothing about living with the reality of a man who's half crippled.'

'Maybe not, but what makes you feel you have the right to deny her the chance to discover if she *can* live with that reality?' asked Sara coolly. 'You're not being fair to her, Sam,' she told her brother. 'If the situation was reversed, would you still love her?'

His immediate, 'Of course,' made him grimace faintly and look at Sara with lifted eyebrows. 'Okay, I get your message, Sara, but the point is . . .'

'The point is that you're letting your pride blind you to the fact that you could be hurting Vanessa more by rejecting her than you ever could by marrying her—I take it it is marriage that's in your mind, and not . . .'

'For God's sake, of course it is!' exploded Sam roughly. 'Just what do you take me for, Sara? She's already had enough bad knocks from life without me adding another. She isn't secure enough in herself to feel happy in a relationship she couldn't feel was permanent.'

'No, she isn't,' Sara agreed. 'Go and telephone her, Sam,' she begged her brother. 'Tell her you've changed your mind and that you'd like her to pick you up after all. Let her make her own decisions about whether or not she can adapt to your way of life— don't make them for her.'

Holding her breath she watched as her brother sat down and reached for the telephone. He knew the number off by heart, she recognised, watching him

punch in the numbers. Vanessa must have answered
the phone; Sam's voice was distinctly husky as he said
her name. Quietly moving out of earshot, Sara left him
to it.

That he hadn't been entirely successful was obvious
the next day when Vanessa drew up outside in her car.

She looked pale, her mouth tight with pain and
tension, and although she longed to reassure her, Sara
felt she could not interfere further. Carly came rushing
down from her room to greet their visitor, flinging
herself enthusiastically into her arms.

'Vanessa's got some teddies just like mine,' she
confided to her aunt. 'And she's going to let me see
them . . .'

'Not today though, I'm afraid.' Vanessa smiled
wanly. 'Today I'm taking your daddy to the hospital.'

Watching from the sidelines, Sara saw that Vanessa
made no attempt to help Sam into the car, refraining
from doing anything that would have brought her in
physical contact with him, and yet despite Vanessa's
aloofness, she was aware of how much the other girl
was suffering.

All women who loved were open to the same pain,
all of her sex sharing a deep in-bred awareness of just
how devastating it could be, Sara thought. It was an
awareness that was seldom mentioned or talked about,
but it was there. She had loved once and known that
pain when tragedy wrenched Rick away from her.
And that was why she was determined never to fall in
love again.

Determined? She stopped with one foot on the
stairs. It wasn't by an effort of will that she couldn't

fall in love, it was because she still loved Rick. Wasn't it?

When Sam and Vanessa returned from the hospital, both of them seemed in much happier spirits. Sam asked Sara if she would mind babysitting Carly for him so that he could take Vanessa out to dinner.

Observing their happiness as they drove away together several hours later, Sara told herself that it wasn't envy that made her own heart heavy with pain. How could she envy Sam and Vanessa what she had sworn she could never experience again?

It was late when they got back, and over supper Sara couldn't help noticing how often they exchanged brief glances and touches. As soon as she decently could she excused herself, fibbing that she was feeling tired.

In fact, she had never felt less like sleep. She was buoyed up by a restless nervy energy that she couldn't seem to dispel. It seemed a long time before she finally heard Vanessa leave. Had Vanessa and her brother been making love?

A shudder of sensation gripped her body, her frantic attempts to summon the protection of Rick's familiar features vanquished by their refusal to form. Instead it was Jonas who filled her thoughts and senses, his mental image tormenting her until she was forced to bury her head beneath her pillows in an attempt to push his intrusive image away.

As the week wore on, Sara found that her mood of nervous tension didn't abate. Whenever she tried to calm herself by thinking of Rick, Jonas's strong features came between her and her memories of her dead love.

Illogically, it was Jonas she blamed for her inability
to remember Rick in exact detail. She was alternately
torn between the feeling that she never wanted to see
him again and the burning need to do so, so that she
could demand that he stop torturing her.

On the Friday evening she babysat for Carly once
again, allowing Vanessa and Sam to go out together.

The thundery weather, which had grown oppres-
sive, drove her to bed early with the beginnings of a
bad headache. The tablets she took beforehand
ensured that she fell asleep almost immediately, but
the physical intensity of her dreams woke her abruptly
within an hour of going to bed.

Her dream had been so real that it was minutes after
she had come awake before she realised that she was
alone in her own bed, that Jonas was not beside her.
Jonas . . . Even though she was alone her body burned,
her skin scorched with heat.

Her dream had been so real that even now she could
hardly comprehend that Jonas wasn't there with her,
that that touch against her skin had not been his but
merely part of her dream.

With returning consciousness came the awareness
of how much her body ached. Pressing her hands to
her breasts, she felt their hard arousal, her throat
suddenly thickening with uncryable tears.

Her headache was even worse than it had been
before, its pounding mirroring the heavy thud of her
pulses. With a tormented cry she got out of bed and
pulled on her wrap, going over to her open casement
window.

Outside the night air was hot and still with the
tension that presages a thunderstorm. After the

thunder would come the relief of rain to freshen the air and release the tension. But there seemed to be no escape for her own tension.

This hectic, almost frantic desire to abandon herself to the physical act of sex was unfamiliar to her. And yet surely she must have experienced this same driving need with Rick? After all, they hadn't been lovers . . . and she had loved him. The fact that she was young and still a virgin had made him very protective and tender towards her, never permitting them to get in a situation that offered too much temptation.

Perhaps it was because she was older that she felt this burning need—or perhaps it was fuelled by the fact that Rick was now lost to her for ever.

As she looked out of her window, she saw a light go on in one of Jonas's greenhouses, and instinctively she withdrew from sight, even though she knew it would be impossible for anyone to see her. Vanessa had said earlier in the week that Jonas was away seeing customers, but now he must be back.

An unwelcome quiver of sensation tormented her skin, raising goosebumps and making her shiver. Why had she dreamed about Jonas—and in such an explicitly sexual way?

Feeling her skin burn once more, she stumbled back to her bed, telling herself that it must have been something to do with the drug she had taken for her headache.

Overnight it rained, the crash of thunder waking Sara briefly in the early hours. When she finally woke it was with the instinctive sensation of having overslept. Quickly showering and dressing, she went downstairs, checking on the threshold of the kitchen when she saw Vanessa deep in conversation with Sam.

'Morning, sleepyhead,' Sam teased, grinning at her. 'Want some coffee?'

'At least a gallon,' Sara confirmed wryly. 'Did you have a good time last night?'

She turned round just in time to see the look her brother and Vanessa exchanged, and was instantly pierced by the most illogical and painful jealousy.

'You could say so,' Sam drawled, fighting to keep the excitement out of his voice and not succeeding at all. 'We're engaged,' he added proudly, lifting Vanessa's hand to his mouth in a gesture so tender and loving that Sara felt her throat almost close up.

'I hope you don't expect me to be surprised,' she managed to say, going forward to hug Vanessa and then kiss her brother.

Oddly enough, it was not the fact that in committing himself to Vanessa Sam was putting the past behind him that made her throat raw and tight, but the knowledge that she and her brother were now on opposite sides of the line that divided those who had love in their lives and those who did not.

She wasn't jealous, she told herself as she watched the tender look Sam and Vanessa exchanged. How could she be? After all, if she had wanted another emotional relationship she could have had one with Jonas . . .

Although it had been the last thing she had intended to say she heard herself commenting brightly to Vanessa, 'I see Jonas is back. The lights were on in one of the greenhouses last night.'

'Yes, he came back just before Sam and I went out. I'm hoping the news of our engagement will put him in a better mood than he's been in these last few days. Something's obviously bothering him, but I don't know what. It isn't like Jonas to be bad-tempered. He's had his problems with the business, but I've never seen him with his temper on as short a fuse as it's on at the moment.'

'It sounds to me as though he needs a woman in his life,' laughed Sam.

'Umm.' Vanessa looked rather grave. 'The parents have been hoping for a long time that he'll marry. My mother worries that his mother's death had such a traumatic effect on him that he won't let himself risk a deep emotional attachment. I can say this to both of you without being disloyal, because you've both experienced the same kind of loss. Jonas hates anyone to think he's anything less than completely invincible, but at heart he's a tremendous romantic. I know when I was pregnant he told me that there was no way he'd ever leave any woman to bear his child alone. Of course that was some time ago, but he's always had a very over-developed sense of responsibility towards others. Perhaps now that I'm off his hands he might start to think seriously about looking for a wife. He needs someone he can share the burden of the house with—and despite its beauty, in many ways it is a burden. It simply eats money on maintenance and upkeep.'

'Obviously what he needs is a very rich wife,' quipped Sara lightly, but Vanessa frowned, her expression very earnest as she said seriously,

'Oh no, Sara, Jonas would never marry just for financial gain. He's very old-fashioned and proud in that way, you know, very much in the same mould as his father.'

'You mean he wants an obedient little homebody of a wife, who'll let him walk all over her?'

Sara could tell by the indignant colour in Vanessa's cheeks that she wasn't pleased.

'I thought you and Jonas liked one another,' she said stiffly, 'but it seems I was wrong. Please forgive me, I shouldn't have bored you with my personal family concerns, Sara.' With a very chilly smile she turned to Sam. 'I'd better get back now, darling. Do you still want to break the news to Carly at lunchtime as we planned or . . .'

'It's all arranged,' Sam told her firmly. 'I've booked a table at The Bull, and I've told Carly it's a very special occasion. I suspect she already has a pretty good idea of what's going to happen. She asked me last night if I thought that God might send her the new mummy she's been praying for soon.'

After he had watched Vanessa drive away Sam turned back from the window and said judicially, 'You were a bit hard on Jonas there, Sara.'

'I'm sorry if I upset Vanessa.' Her voice was toneless, but in reality she felt extremely guilty. Vanessa's quiet reaction to her comments had made her feel very uncomfortable and bad-mannered.

'She's a very fond sister,' was Sam's only comment, although he added, 'and you should know what that means. I must say though, that, like her, I thought you and he were getting on pretty well.'

'You mean you thought there might be another romance brewing,' snapped Sara. 'That would be nice and tidy, wouldn't it? But I'm not like you, Sam—I can't bring myself to forget the past and start afresh.'

'Now just a minute.' Looking very angry, Sam hobbled towards her, gripping her arm. 'If you're trying to insinuate that because I'm marrying Vanessa, Holly and my life with her will be completely forgotten, you couldn't be more wrong. Vanessa and I are both agreed that we want Carly to grow up feeling that she can talk freely about her mother. Holly was a very important part of my life before I met Vanessa, and she will always have a place in my heart. The fact that I'm marrying Vanessa doesn't mean I'm trying to wipe out the past. I love Vanessa in a very different way than I loved Holly. She and I were young together; neither of us had experienced the pain that both Vanessa and I have experienced. It will be a different relationship—a *different* relationship, Sara, not a better or a worse one, simply a different one. You know, you're clinging so hard to the past that I'm beginning to wonder why you're so frightened to let it go. This isn't the life Rick would have wanted for you . . .'

'How do you know what Rick would have wanted for me?'

It shocked her to hear herself practically screaming the words.

'I know because he was my friend a damn sight longer than he was your fiancé,' Sam returned, equally incensed. 'I've sat back and watched while you've put him on a pedestal, Sara, but I'm telling you now that the Rick you seem to have enshrined in your memories bears precious little resemblance to the Rick I knew; he was a living, breathing human being, not a demi-god.'

'Stop it; I don't want to listen to any more!' Covering her ears, Sara ran out of the room, not stopping until she had reached the sanctuary of her own bedroom.

As she sank down on the bed, she chided herself for her adolescent behaviour. It was all Jonas's fault, she thought tormentedly. Until he came into her life she had been quite content, and now . . .

Now she ached with an unsatisfied sexual need that tormented her mentally nearly as much as it did physically. It seemed incomprehensible that she should be subject to this fierce tug of physical desire, a desire so strong that it made her jumpy and short-tempered, that it tricked her into quarrelling with Sam and upsetting Vanessa. With a low moan she buried her head in her hands. Perhaps the only way she was going to get rid of it was to succumb to it. Shocked by what she was being forced to admit, she got up and walked over to the window.

Carly was playing outside in the garden with the dog. When Sam and Vanessa married there would be no place here for her. She would have to find somewhere else to live . . . and some means of supporting herself.

Soon Vanessa would be returning to pick Sam and Carly up for their luncheon date. She glanced at her watch. There was plenty of time to get Carly washed and ready; like Sam, she did not anticipate any problems with the little girl accepting Vanessa as her stepmother. Already she had shown how much she liked Vanessa, and Vanessa herself was not the type to differentiate between her stepdaughter and any other children she and Sam might have.

She would go downstairs and bring Carly in to get her ready, but first she had to make her peace with Sam.

Squaring her shoulders, she went down to his sitting-room. It was easier than she had expected. He was as eager to make up their quarrel as she was.

'I'm sorry if I upset you,' he apologised gruffly. 'But since I've met Vanessa I've begun to realise what you're doing to yourself, Sara. You're turning yourself into a nun, living life only at third-hand. That isn't what Rick would have wanted for you. I know that . . .'

'Maybe it's what I want for myself,' responded Sara lightly, but he refused to be mollified.

'If it is you're motivated purely by cowardice,' he told her bluntly. 'You won't let yourself make a commitment to another man because you're afraid. Don't think I don't realise that, or that I don't sympathise, but try to see what you're doing to yourself!'

'We could argue about this for the rest of our lives, Sam, and still remain on opposite sides of the fence. You've chosen your way of life and you must leave me to choose mine. I'll go out and get Carly and get her ready. You deserve to be happy,' she told him quietly, 'and I'm sorry if I seemed churlish. I know that marrying Vanessa doesn't mean you've forgotten Holly.'

'No, it doesn't, any more than you marrying someone else would mean that you've forgotten Rick.'

He saw the shuttered look close her face and sighed. 'Okay, from now on we'll consider the subject taboo, but there is one final thing I want to add, Sara.

Vanessa and I are both agreed that you'll always have
a home here.'

He might say that now, but Sara knew that there
would come a time when her brother would want his
wife and family to himself. However, there was no
point in discussing it now.

'When do you plan to get married?' she asked
instead.

'As soon as possible. Neither of us see any point in
waiting. Of course there could be a problem in that
Jonas will have to find someone to take over Vanessa's
job. I don't suppose you'd fancy giving it a try?'

'No way,' Sara told him firmly. Work for Jonas?
She shuddered at the very thought!

CHAPTER SEVEN

THE thunder which she had expected would clear the air hadn't been totally effective, and a slumbrous stillness permeated the atmosphere when Sara walked round the garden a little later on.

She was leaning over the fence, talking to the donkey, when she heard Vanessa's car. Its doors slammed and then she saw the flash of sunlight bouncing off the glass as Sam opened the French window, Vanessa coming out after him.

She was hidden from them by one of the overgrown rhododendron bushes that someone had planted to screen the paddock from the garden, but it was obvious that she had waited a little too long to answer Sam's call, Sara realised in dismay as she stepped away from the fence and saw her brother take Vanessa in his arms.

There was nothing tentative or hesitant about the way they kissed, and the sight of them lost to everything but their blind need for one another invoked such a terrible tearing agony of deprivation inside her that she was half-way down the garden before she realised that she was running.

It was an indication of how engrossed they were in each other that neither Vanessa nor Sam seemed to have heard her noisy flight. She could hardly go back now, she thought numbly—at least not without embarrassing both herself and Vanessa. She had never considered herself prudish, but there was something particularly intimate about the kiss she had unwittingly observed, and all she knew was that she wouldn't have wanted anyone else to witness her kissing and being kissed so passionately.

At the bottom of the garden where it touched the boundary fence of Jonas's land was a heavy wooden gate. Biting her lip, Sara turned the handle and stepped through it.

Beyond the rough grass that edged the fence lay several very large polythene growing tunnels. Edging her way between them, Sara went in search of a path that would lead her back to the road that ran past the cottage. That way, she could get back without either Sam or Vanessa being aware that they had been observed. If they asked where she had been she could always tell them that she had gone for a walk.

Deeply engrossed in her thoughts, she was unaware of Jonas's cat-like progress towards her until she almost cannoned into him. The shock of seeing him, on top of the turmoil she had already experienced, thoroughly shocked her, the colour draining out of her face as she stepped back warily.

'Careful; the path is a bit rocky here.'

The sensation of Jonas's fingers on her arm disturbed her. The sleeves of his checked shirt were rolled up to the elbows, revealing the lean muscularity of his arms. He had nice arms, she thought absently, neither too brawny nor lacking in muscle.

The trickle of sensation curling down her spine as she fought back the impulse to touch his skin with her

fingers threw her completely off balance, and she
tugged away from Jonas's restraining hand more out
of fear of her own emotions than resentment of his
touching her.

As she stepped back her heel missed the cinder
path, and she overbalanced wildly, falling heavily on
her left ankle. The pain that shot through it was so
excruciating that she couldn't hold back a shocked
cry.

The next moment Jonas was down on his knees in
front of her, his fingers running capably and gently
over her rapidly swelling flesh.

'You haven't broken it. It's just a sprain.'

Looking down on him while he kneeled at her feet
was the oddest sensation; something akin to tender-
ness welled up inside her. She almost reached out to
touch the soft thickness of his dark hair, but
fortunately common sense stopped her.

'I'll have to carry you up to the house,' he said. 'That
ankle will need bathing, and you can't put any weight
on it.'

She was in his arms before she could find the breath
to protest, the sudden insecurity of finding herself
above the ground making her cling instinctively to
him, her hands locking behind his neck.

This close, she could smell the scent of his skin. A
soft sheen of perspiration dampened his throat, and
where her fingers rested against his back, his shirt
stuck to his skin.

One arm supported her beneath her knees, the other
resting against her midriff just below the curve of her
breast.

Outside the back door, Jonas balanced her against his thigh as he pushed open the door. The ripples of quicksilver heat that darted through her as she felt his muscles compacting in a subtle reminder of his masculinity infuriated her, all the more so because she knew quite well that there was nothing in the least provocative in his movements, and that he was simply reacting instinctively to a minor crisis. A crisis which he would have handled in exactly the same way whatever her sex.

'I'll take you upstairs so that I can have a look at your ankle,' he told her as he carried her through the kitchen, nudging the door open with his shoulder. His movements brought his fingers into a more intimate contact with her breast, and the sudden ache of need that shocked through her made her catch her breath.

'What's wrong? Did I jolt you? It won't be long now. I want to make sure that the skin isn't broken; those cinders can be lethal if they get embedded.'

'Then why use them?' Sara asked him tartly, glad of something to cling on to to distract her from the effect of their intimacy.

'Mainly because they happen to be cheap. Luckily we don't get many people wandering along them in high heels,' he added sardonically. 'Since I can't imagine that you were looking for me, what exactly was it you were looking for?'

As he shouldered open one of the bedroom doors, Sara bit her lip in vexation. She could hardly tell him the truth.

'I was just curious to see what lay on the other side of our fence,' she lied.

The room looked like a guest room, the bedspread pristine smooth and the furniture highly polished.

'I brought you in here because this room has its own bathroom,' Jonas told her, dropping her carelessly on to the bed. 'If you hang on a minute, I'll go into my own bathroom and bring back some iodine and a bandage.' He paused and eyed her sardonically. 'Curious, were you? Strange,' he scoffed mockingly. 'Curiosity—about anything—would be the very last thing I'd expect from you.'

Sara knew that he was deliberately taunting her, and the taunt stung, but she kept her eyes averted, trying not to wince as he dropped down on his haunches beside her, carefully taking her foot between his hands.

'Mmm . . . the skin doesn't seem to be grazed, but we'll get it cleaned up and then take another look. Don't go away,' he drawled mockingly, getting up and heading for the door.

He was only gone for ten minutes at the most, but it was long enough for Sara to have edged her way restlessly off the bed, and to have started moving in an awkward crab-like motion towards the door.

It opened inward just as she reached it, the curse that left Jonas's lips making her flinch.

'What is it about you?' he demanded irefully. 'Just where in hell's name did you think you were going?'

'To find a telephone. Sam and Vanessa will be wondering where I am.'

'Stop worrying; they know. I rang the cottage while I was in my room and told Sam what had happened. I'll run you back there later when we get that ankle strapped up. I'm afraid this is going to hurt,' he warned her, depositing the tray he was carrying on the bedside chest. It contained a bowl of water, some iodine and cotton wool, a bandage and a nearly full bottle of brandy. 'It will help take the edge off the shock and the physical pain,' said Jonas, seeing her look at the brandy. 'Here, drink this.'

The glass he poured her seemed far too generous. Sara rarely touched spirits, not liking the taste, and she grimaced as the fierce heat of the brandy bit into her throat.

'Don't sip it, drink it,' Jonas directed, watching her grimly. Already she could feel her head beginning to spin, a reminder that as yet today she had had nothing to eat, and yet, sensing that if she proved obdurate he would force the stuff down her throat, Sara reluctantly drained the glass.

'Good girl.' Jonas crouched down beside her again, one hand holding her ankle while the other explored it gently. As he touched the tender area where it was swollen, Sara winced. 'These jeans are going to have to come off. If you can stand the loss I suggest I cut them free—that will be the least painful method of removing them.'

The jeans in question were the cropped type that finished above the ankle, snugly hugging the shape of her leg, and the thought of tugging them off over her tender skin made Sara grimace.

She watched in silence as Jonas wielded the scissors in a businesslike fashion, cutting up the outside seam to her waistband. Underneath her jeans she was wearing a pair of minuscule cotton briefs, and her

shocked, protesting attempt to cover herself with the
denim as Jonas casually pushed the fabric aside and
proceeded to tug her ruined jeans off her uninjured leg
made him pause and stare at her uncomprehendingly.

'What the devil's the matter?' he demanded grimly,
his mouth suddenly relaxing into an unforgivably
amused curve as he told her softly, 'I *have* seen a
woman's body before, you know.'

'But not mine,' Sara snapped back shortly. It
unsettled her seeing him in this distant, almost cool
mood. When he picked her up outside she had steeled
herself against further passionate declarations of his
feelings for her, but instead he was treating her as
though she were almost a complete stranger.

For some reason her ire seemed to increase his
amusement; his smile deepened, and Sara fought
against acknowledging how attractive he looked with
that teasing glint in his eyes, his stance, as he leaned
over the bed towards her, subtly emphasising the
smooth hardness of his body.

What on earth was the matter with her? Sara chided
herself. There was no reason at all for her to be aware
of him like this; he was not aware of her in the same
way; he was not disturbed by her proximity, or by the
sensation of her breath against his skin as he leaned
across her to tug away the disputed jeans. Whereas she
. . . She swallowed numbly, trying to deny the effect he
was having on her, but the sensation curling hotly
through her stomach refused to go away. She wanted
to reach out and touch him, to breathe in the smell of
his skin, to . . .

In fact she was so deeply caught up in her battle

against the effect he was having on her senses that when he drawled softly, 'Radically different, is it, or is it simply that no mere human male can be permitted to look upon the body once possessed by Saint Richard?' initially the import of his sarcastic comment was almost lost on her. And then abruptly she realised what he had said, and her skin burned with an anger that was heightened by her own knowledge of just how ambivalent her feelings towards him actually were.

It was obviously true that it was possible to feel desire without love—without even liking, she thought bitterly, wondering wryly what he would say if he knew that her reluctance to part with her jeans sprang from her own awareness of her vulnerability towards him. No doubt he would be extremely amused, especially after the way she had rejected him.

But as she had told him then, it was merely a sexual attraction she felt for him; the fascination of the moth for the flame, she thought angrily, that part of the human nature that is relentlessly drawn towards that which it knows will do it the least good.

The touch of Jonas's fingers against her skin as he deftly cleaned and then bandaged her swollen ankle was cool and clinical. He hadn't even so much as glanced at her body, never mind evinced any of the uncontrolled passion she had sensed in him the night he told her he was falling in love with her.

A combination of shock and alcohol, plus lack of food, was making her feel distinctly drowsy. Her head suddenly seemed to be too heavy for her neck, and found its way automatically on to the softness of a down pillow. She was aware of her ankle being released and of missing the human warmth of another's touch against her skin. She tried to protest, but the words became a thick, unintelligible blur on her tongue. She was conscious of movement within the room, of the light gently being shut out, and then there was nothing but a deep, dark pit of welcoming sleep.

She climbed reluctantly out of it some time later, conscious of being forced to part from a dream that had been intensely pleasurable. In it, she had not been lying alone, she thought drowsily; someone else had been with her, holding her, touching her . . . Rick, of course . . . No, not Rick. Rick had been in her dream but he had been an irritant, a barrier which stood between her and the man whose arms she so desperately wanted around her. The man. What man? Jonas!

Like tiny ripples quickly growing on the stillness of a millpond, the shock spread outwards through her body, until she was confused by what was reality and what was not. Her head felt muzzy, her thoughts disordered and vague. Her ankle ached, but not badly. The room was unfamiliar to her, the curtains making it dark and clothing unfamiliar objects in deep shadows.

Gradually reality crept back. She had been dreaming about Jonas, dreaming that Jonas was making love to her, but then Rick had come between them, and Jonas had gone away from her. She shuddered deeply, caught up in a fierce spiral of physical desire. She tried desperately to cling to the fading image of Rick, but, like a talisman that had lost its power, his features no longer had the ability to blot Jonas out of her mind.

Instead, Jonas's were the features that formed within her skull, his the touch she remembered against her skin. Jonas's touch . . . impossible, and yet there was no denying the very real ache deep inside her, the almost gnawing need she had to be kissed and caressed by his mouth and hands.

Beneath the bedspread she moved restlessly, trying to escape from what her body was telling her, her hand accidentally catching the heavy lamp beside the bed and sending it crashing to the floor.

Luckily it was unharmed, but Sara was still crouching on the floor, looking at it, when the bedroom door was thrust open and Jonas strode in.

'I'm sorry . . . I woke up and knocked the lamp over.'

How constrained and tense she sounded! She dared not look at Jonas in case he should somehow divine her state of mind.

'I've no idea what time it is,' she said jerkily, keeping her back to him, trying to fill the thick silence with something . . . anything that would stop her from turning round and throwing herself into his arms. What on earth was wrong with her? She didn't love him . . . she didn't even like him. But she wanted him. Oh God, how she wanted him! Crouching here on the floor, she only had to close her eyes to feel the satin-smooth glide of his skin against her own, to taste the hot savagery of his kiss, to . . .

'It isn't that late. You've been asleep for an hour or so, that's all. By the way,' he added casually, 'Sam rang and suggested you spend the night here.' When she made no comment he added drily, 'I dare say that's more for his sake than yours. He and Vanessa don't get many opportunities to be alone.'

'You know they're getting married?'

She kept her voice low so that he wouldn't hear the panic in it. She was to stay the night. Oh God, how on earth was she going to endure it? She barely recognised herself in the woman she had suddenly become, a woman who ached so much for the physical possession of the man standing behind her that it took a concentrated effort of will not to stand up and beg him to make love to her.

'Yes.' His voice was clipped, giving her no indication of his feelings on the subject, although his curt, 'What will you do when they do?' reminded her that she couldn't rely on having a home with her brother for ever, no matter what he might say.

Turning round and standing up slowly, like an old person, she said carefully, 'I'm not sure. Go back to London, I suppose. I'll have a better chance of finding a job there.'

He swore so unexpectedly and graphically that she swayed where she stood, grabbing hold of the bed as she inadvertently put her weight on her bad ankle.

It all happened so quickly, Jonas's arms coming round her to support her, that she wasn't sure if he had cursed first, or if she had stumbled.

'You shouldn't be out of bed,' he told her harshly.

A tremor of intense excitement ran liquid heat through her veins, the pleasure of having him so close to her so intoxicating that it blinded her to everything else. In a voice she barely recognised as her own, she whispered provocatively, 'Then you'll just have to put me back, won't you.'

She felt the tension grip his muscles in the same second as it hit her what she was doing. And then the panic that clutched at her stomach was gone as she remembered what he had said about not wanting merely sex from her. It must surely be her overcharged imagination that told her that the intensely passionate look in his eyes meant anything, but when he slid his hands slowly down her bare arms, and asked huskily, 'Does that mean what I think it means?' she wondered if she hadn't been extremely foolish after all.

It bemused her that she, who had managed to stay so sensible and controlled in Rick's arms, should feel this irresistible urge to abandon common sense completely whenever Jonas touched her. And when he touched her the way he was doing now, the merest stroking of his fingertips against the quiveringly sensitive flesh of her inner arms, she felt as though she would rather die than let him stop what he was doing to her.

'I want you to make love to me.'

She could hardly credit that she had actually said the words, until she felt the sudden slam of Jonas's heart against his ribs, its fierce kick registered by her own muscles.

'Do you *know* what you're saying to me? No, don't bother answering that,' he said thickly as he dragged her into his arms and held her there.

As she felt the heat coming off his body, reality intruded sharply into her dream world and she tensed, saying huskily, 'I thought you didn't want this. That you didn't want sex from me . . .'

'Is that what I said?' He held her slightly away from him, looking down into her eyes with a faintly brooding expression while his hands cupped her face, his fingers stroking behind her ears and down her throat.

His mouth hovered close to hers, and, shamingly, Sara knew that she wanted its heat and possession, to the extent that she was quite wantonly urging her body forward, and parting her lips.

She heard him groan as his mouth closed over hers, the sound intensely exciting. One of them was shaking, or was it both of them?

'Perhaps you're right after all,' he muttered, taking his mouth momentarily from hers. 'Perhaps it *is* just sex. You'll have to overlook my foolish romantic yearnings; they obviously blinded me to reality.'

Was that bitterness or contempt that ran through his voice like a thread of steel?

'Whatever it is between us, I know that you find it as irresistible as I do, don't you?'

His teeth were taking tiny little bites at her lower lip, his tongue stroking and touching, its erotic movements driving her into a delirium of desire.

'Yes . . . Yes . . .' She heard the hoarse moan as though it had been made by someone else, but at least he had acknowledged now that it was simply sex between them; that made it easier for her to endure the fierce need that burned inside her. Wanting him in a purely sexual way was not a betrayal of Rick.

'And sex is all you want from me, isn't it?'

The harshness of his voice momentarily broke through her arousal. Blinking warily at him as she focused on the grey heat of his eyes, she said unsteadily, 'I don't want anything from you.'

The sound he made deep in his throat made her shiver, her muscles clenching, as his hands slid up under her tee-shirt, uncovering her breasts, his hands cupping them as he rubbed his thumbs slowly against her hard nipples.

'Liar,' he whispered rawly against her ear. 'You want this.' Her response to the deliberate intimacy of his thumbs against her sensitive skin made him laugh softly. 'And this . . .' His mouth found hers, touching and teasing her parted lips, until with a small moan of need she flung her arms round him and dragged his head down so that she could fasten her mouth on his.

For a few seconds he stayed passive beneath her feverish assault, and then, momentarily lifting his mouth from hers, he muttered thickly, 'And so, God help me, do I!'

She couldn't stop her body vibrating with a shudder of pleasure when he started to kiss her, his mouth fiercely demanding that she held nothing back, warning that if she didn't give him the response he sought he would take it anyway.

It was nothing like the tender kisses she had shared with Rick; nothing like them at all, and to her shame she found that beneath the pressure of Jonas's mouth she felt more a woman than she had felt at any other time in her life.

They kissed with a famished need that a minute detached part of her brain registered with awe. It was alien to her personality to react like this. She had always enjoyed Rick's gentle lovemaking, but she had never felt any urge to take it beyond the limits he set on it; she had been content to let Rick set the pace, but now she knew that if Jonas were to stop touching her she would use every bit of feminine power she had to make him want her.

Just then she felt him move away from her, his breathing harshly unsteady against her ear as he levered himself upright.

Before she could speak he said thickly, 'Too many clothes.' And in the semi-light filtering through the closed curtains Sara watched him tug off his shirt and jeans.

His body was every bit as masculine as she had imagined, her fingers trembling slightly as she touched the sharp ridge of his spine. His skin felt hot, his muscles clenching as her hand slid round to his hip. He was wearing a pair of white briefs which he also tugged off and dropped on the floor before coming back to her.

It seemed ridiculous that she had reached the grand old age of twenty-five without ever seeing the male body so intimately before. She had seen Rick in his swimming things, of course, but, minimal though they had been, it wasn't the same. There was something primitive, and even a little threatening, about the strong, clean line of Jonas's body as he turned back towards her and was caught momentarily in the half light.

A dark ribbon of hair curled down the centre of his torso, spreading and thickening where it reached the top of his thighs. His arousal was so obvious that Sara automatically averted her eyes, feeling her skin flush with heat. But the heat wasn't caused by embarrassment. She ached to reach out and touch him, to reassure herself that he was real, that his desire for her was real, and not just a continuation of her earlier dream.

'Don't look at me like that.' His voice was raw and unsteady, causing her to tense and look up into his face.

Had she done something wrong? 'Why not?'

Her own voice was huskily unfamiliar, sharing the tension she had heard in his.

'Because it makes me ache to feel your hands against my skin,' Jonas groaned into her ear as he leaned forwards to take her in his arms.

She was still wearing her tee-shirt, and she twisted instinctively within his embrace, wanting to be rid of it, wanting to be rid of anything that came between their two skins.

'You want to take this off?' His voice was hot and thick, making her shiver in hectic excitement, the erotically rough abrasion of his body hair against her midriff as he leaned into her making her gasp in pleasure.

As he had done before he slid his hands up under her tee-shirt, cupping her breasts. Her nipples were already hard and taut, pushing eagerly against the soft cotton, and when he bent his head and started to tease the twin spirals through the fabric of her tee-shirt Sara thought she would go mad with the frenzy of pleasure inside her.

Held captive by the superior weight of his body, she could only move her head protestingly from side to side and pluck impatiently at her tee-shirt as she tried to convey her need to have his mouth against her body without anything between them.

But Jonas seemed to be enjoying teasing her, keeping up his deliberate torment until the cotton clung to her skin in damp transparency. She had never experienced anything so erotic in all her life, and she shuddered protestingly beneath the slow caress of his tongue.

The skin on his hands was slightly rough, and where it touched her breasts beneath her tee-shirt, the delicate friction fed her growing desire for something more than his light caress.

Just when she felt she could not bear it any longer, Jonas moved swiftly, dragging her tee-shirt over her head and flinging it on to the floor, his mouth finding the hot pink crest of one nipple and tugging on it fiercely with a smothered groan of satisfaction.

As though an electric current passed through her body from that point of contact Sara found herself arching frantically against him, her head thrown back, the muscles in her throat cording as she raked her nails over his back.

She wanted him desperately Sara acknowledged, her body bathed in a heat that matched his own, as she moved instinctively beneath him and felt the shudder of need rip through his muscles as his hands slid to her hips, lifting her slightly, supporting her, caressing her.

Her thighs parted instinctively to accommodate him, her legs lifting eagerly to wrap round him as she welcomed the first smooth thrust of his body against and then within her own.

Despite the fact that he was her first lover there was no pain, just the merest pang of discomfort, but she thought he would not notice.

But despite the intensity of his arousal and desire, he did notice, checking slightly, his mouth leaving her throat as his eyes narrowed on hers, asking the question she could see forming on his lips.

Instinctively Sara placed her fingers against his mouth, letting her body tell him how much it welcomed and wanted him, her eyes widening with shock and excitement as she felt him move inside her.

Her fingertips still rested against his mouth. His lips parted, his tongue touching the soft pink pads, his teeth nipping delicately before he sucked her fingers into the moist heat of his mouth, his movements mirroring the erotic responsiveness of her body to his possession.

Heat bathed her body, her skin breaking out in a moist show of perspiration. His mouth released her fingers, his tongue touching the hollow of her throat, absorbing the tiny bead of sweat gathering there.

The urgency which gripped and drove her now was like nothing she had ever experienced before, the compulsion so great that she could barely comprehend the magnitude of it. Nothing mattered but the need to satisfy the urgent rhythm of his body, to ...

As her senses started to explode in concentric spasms of pleasure she cried out unintelligibly, shuddering as she felt Jonas tense, his breathing ragged and hoarse, the sound of her name on his lips almost unfamiliar to her as he reached his own physical release.

Drowsily she decided it must be shock and weakness that made her cuddle up instinctively into the warmth of Jonas's body as he carefully eased himself away from her, and gently stroked her tired limbs.

She heard him say her name and tried to open her eyes, but they felt as though lead weights were attached to them. She gave an inarticulate murmur, but was too exhausted to stay awake.

As she slid fathoms deep into sleep she was vaguely aware of the dull throb of her ankle—something she had totally forgotten while Jonas was making love to her—and of the delicious warmth of his body, its protective bulk curled around her.

CHAPTER EIGHT

SHE woke up slowly, warm with languorous pleasure, half reluctant to leave sleep behind and yet knowing that something better awaited her.

The name that murmured past her lips as she reached out to touch the man beside her belonged to the past, and she knew it, but the intensity of the physical pleasure she had experienced with Jonas had been so overpowering that she was still half in shock. It was easier, and much, much safer, to pretend that it was Rick who had made love to her and not Jonas.

She had thought Jonas was asleep and that there was no one other than herself to hear her self-indulgent lie, but the moment Rick's name was whispered past her lips she knew she was wrong.

Strong fingers bit into her arms as Jonas turned over, pushing her back against the bed and holding her there, one hand momentarily leaving her arm to snap on the bedside lamp.

'So that's it, is it? You were using me as a stand-in,' he said hoarsely. 'Damn you, Sara—but I should have guessed, shouldn't I? You'd never have given your precious virginity to me, would you?'

He was barely speaking above a whisper, but she was frighteningly aware of his anger. His mouth, the mouth that had kissed and caressed her skin to such a pitch that it still tingled slightly, was now curled in a vicious snarl of rage, his eyes as cold and empty as a winter landscape.

She sensed that he was using his anger to mask the blow she had struck to his pride, but instead of pleasing her, all she could feel was a vast aching well of emptiness, because she had not pretended he was Rick when he was making love to her. She had known exactly who was holding her in his arms, touching her ... loving her. A terrible tearing pain threatened to wrench her body apart as the truth hit her. Despite everything she had taught herself, despite all the barriers she had built up against him, despite the fact that he was now looking at her as though he would like nothing better than to choke her to death, she had fallen in love with Jonas.

For a second her shock was so intense that she thought she was going to black out, her first panicky thought being that whatever else happened Jonas must not discover how she felt. If he did ... Not so very long ago he had told her he was on the verge of falling in love with her and she had rejected him; she wasn't going to give him the opportunity to reject her in the same way.

And if he didn't reject her ... if he did genuinely love her ... It made no difference, she reminded herself. After Rick's death she had made her decision never to leave herself vulnerable to the agony of loving and losing someone ever again, and she intended to stick to that decision.

Yes, it was better that Jonas continued to think she had pretended he was Rick, she told herself stoically, gritting her teeth as she felt him shake her as though he wanted to shake the damning words out of her.

'What sort of man was he, anyway?' he demanded thickly, starting down at her in bitter dislike. 'Why did he never make love to you, Sara? Wasn't he capable of . . .'

The sound of her open palm hitting his face startled them both; Sara felt the reverberation of the blow shudder through her body, her eyes closing against the blazing anger she saw in Jonas.

'Don't you dare say a word against Rick!' she heard herself stammering wildly. 'He loved me and he respected me. We weren't lovers because there wasn't time . . .'

She knew that the anguish in her voice was as much for what she considered her own betrayal of Rick's memory in loving Jonas as it was for what Jonas was saying. She knew now with the experience that Jonas had given her, with the knowledge of the intensity of physical love that Jonas had shown her, that Rick must have seen her more as a cherished child than an adult woman. And hadn't that just been what Sam had been trying so gently to tell her during these past weeks?

With an anguished moan of pain, she tried to wrench free of Jonas's grip and bury her face in the pillow, but he wouldn't let her; his voice was thick with anger as his fingers tightened round her arms. 'Oh, no, you don't . . . I'm not your precious Rick, content to behave like some bloodless hero out of a children's story book. I'm a flesh and blood man, Sara, with all the failings and needs that the words imply. So you thought it was Rick who was making love to you, did you?' he demanded with a soft venom that was somehow more frightening than his earlier anger. 'Well, then, this time I'd better make sure you know exactly who it is you're holding in your arms, hadn't I? Hadn't I?' he reiterated gratingly, giving her a little shake.

Sara couldn't think past his ominous 'this time'. Did he mean to make love to her again, then? A tiny shock of fear tensed her spine, a betraying tingle of excitement heating her blood.

He moved—not quickly, but with a slow deliberation that held all the frightening grace and beautiful menace of a panther moving in on its prey.

While her heart and pulses leapt with something that was not entirely fear, her body registered the satin heat of Jonas's against it, the hard length of his leg pinning her to the bed, the slow, insolent movement of his hand as it slid from her arm to her wrist and from there to her waist and her hip, finally coming to rest on the quivering vulnerability of her stomach.

'Now,' he demanded softly. 'Tell me that you know who I am. Say my name.'

The soft words rippled against her ear, as innocent as a wave caressing the beach, but waves could be dangerous, treacherous, and Sara felt her body tremble in apprehension as it recognised the will-power cloaked by the gentle whisper.

She found she was swallowing, her throat tight with nerves, tight and dry, far too dry for her to say anything.

'Say it. Say my name.'

He wasn't even watching her now; instead his

attention seemed to have strayed to her body, his voice deceptively light and expressionless. His hand moved, making the nerve endings under her skin pulse and flutter.

Drawn against her will to watch what he was doing, Sara saw his hand stroke from her stomach up to her breast.

Hot colour sprang into her cheeks as she saw the way her nipples hardened in exultant anticipation of his touch.

'Your body wants me, doesn't it, Sara? *He* never possesed it, never taught it the pleasure of which it was capable. You want *me*.'

She had intended to deny it, to fight him every inch of the way, so whose was this voice that ached and cracked with longing?

'Yes ... Yes ...'

His hand had reached her breast now, sliding warmly beneath it, cupping it so that she could feel the faint callouses against her more tender skin. He moved, dipping his head, and her whole body quivered in anticipation of the sensation of his mouth against her breast.

Little shock waves of mingled arousal and frustration exploded through her as he murmured, a breath away from her skin, 'Yes, *who*, Sara?'

Like Shylock, he wanted to extract every last ounce of retribution, to wring from her payment in full for letting him think she had pretended he was Rick.

And the longer she withheld his victory from him, the more he would make her pay. Every second that ticked past accrued interest on the debt, and she shivered again. Not in desire this time, but in despair, sensing the abyss opening up in front of her. To admit that it was Jonas who aroused her body, who made her ache and cry out for fulfilment, was to lay herself open to unimaginable pain, but if she refused, if she pretended she was not in the least affected by the warm pressure of his hand against her breast, or by the promise implied by the proximity of his mouth and its moist heat, then he would go on and on, until she was forced to concede.

Surely it was better to give in now, while she still had some last remnants of self-control, when she could get away with admitting merely that sexually she found him desirable? If she withheld that admission, who knew what she might be driven to betray to him in the intense paroxysm of pleasure she knew all too well he could drive her to?

And yet one part of her wanted that from him, wanted him to make slow and languorous love to her until both of them melted in the fierce heat of culmination, until neither of them had the willpower to resist the force they had built together.

Sanity urged the former course. Swallowing against the dryness in her throat, she whispered huskily, 'Yes, Jonas.'

She went limp with relief as his hand left her breast, and yet part of her ached for him to go on touching her. He moved, rolling his weight off her body, but as she made to scramble away his arms came round her, securing her against him, taking her with him as he moved so that she lay sprawled on top of him, chest to chest, unable to even take a breath without becoming excruciatingly aware of him.

'What are you doing? You got what you wanted.'

Panic made her voice high and tremulous, the deep sound of the laughter rocking his chest making her tense, her eyes widening on his face.

'I'm not as easily satisfied as your precious Rick,' he told her mockingly. 'That was just a small foretaste of what I want from you, my lovely.'

She saw then that he had just been playing with her, that nothing less than her total subjugation would satisfy the blow she had struck his ego, and she began to fight against his imprisoning arms, gasping out in panic as she felt them tighten round her, effortlessly constraining her, every frantic movement of her body serving only to enforce on her the masculinity of his.

He waited until she was breathing in harsh sobs of exhaustion before saying softly, 'Now we'll begin. Say after me, I want you, Jonas.'

The words stuck in her throat, held prisoner there not so much by fear but by the awful realisation of how true they were. She did want him; shamingly, shockingly so.

Logic and sanity were ignored now. Something more primitive ruled her senses. Her mouth locking in a hard line of denial, she turned her head away.

'Cat got your tongue, has it? Maybe this will help.'

He moved, and she had to tense every muscle against the slow exploration of his mouth as it caressed her throat, its pressure subtly increasing until he reached the pulse at its base. The sensation of his mouth closing over it and sucking her skin in a rhythm that quickly matched the frantic throbbing of her vein made her go weak with longing, but she still refused to give in.

'Well, if that didn't appeal to you, perhaps you'd prefer this . . .'

Not appeal to her? Sara shuddered as his mouth left her throat. He knew exactly what he was doing to her; she had betrayed herself physically even if she had remained silent verbally.

His hands gripped her waist, lifting her slightly. Still fighting for breath, she looked down at him, suppressing a sharp cry of denial as she saw his tongue stroke teasingly against her nipple.

Over and over again he repeated the light caress, first on one breast and then on the other, until she was shivering with a mixture of arousal and anguish. She raised her hands to push herself away from him and instead found that she was curling her fingers into his skin, scarring its surface with her nails as her spine arched in involuntary ecstasy, her breasts swollen and eager for the heat of his mouth.

When he stopped touching her she shivered convulsively, unable to stop herself looking down at her body. Her nipples throbbed deeply pink; her skin was flushed and still faintly moist from his tongue.

'Say it.'

The words whispered invitingly against her skin, tormenting and tantalising her as she watched the movement of his mouth and then heard herself saying as though she had no will of her own, 'I want you, Jonas.'

'And this, you want this. Tell me, Sara.'

His mouth closed over her breast, gentle at first as

he caressed her swollen nipple and then more demanding as he felt her shuddering response.

'God, yes ... Yes ...' Barely aware of speaking, Sara arched her back, inviting him to do with her whatever he wished.

His mouth found the valley between her breasts and teased the tiny bead of sweat forming there, his hands sliding to her hips and then her thighs, moving her so that she straddled him. His skin felt hot against her own, burning into her.

'And this. You want this?'

His voice wasn't as cool or as steady now, but Sara had all but forgotten what had first precipitated his touch. When his fingers stroked softly against her body, seeking and then finding the intimate feminine core of her, she cried out in pleasure, pressing eagerly against his caress, finding relief from the frantic tension building up inside her by burying her mouth against his shoulder. Her tongue tasted the salt tang of his sweat, and found it enjoyed the maleness of him, her hands eagerly caressing his skin as she tried to stifle her whimpers of pleasure against his throat.

'Say it. Say that it's me you want.'

Say it? Didn't he know? Couldn't he tell?

'I want you. I want you, Jonas.' The words, once said, seemed to pour out of her as though they had previously been dammed, words that had no meaning save that they formed a litany that told him of her pleasure and her desire, his name interspersed with her sharp high cries of need.

The world exploded in a spasm of pleasure that tore his name from her throat; her body was reluctant to lose contact with his as he gently rolled her over on to her back.

As he leaned over her, she reached up and touched his face, her eyes closed, her fingers drifting down his throat. His skin was slick with sweat, like her own. He had given her so much pleasure, but he . . .

Her hand slid down his body.

'No!'

The harsh denial in his voice as he captured her fingers shocked her into opening her eyes. His face was flushed, his eyes brilliant with arousal. He wanted her, didn't he?

She glanced at his body covertly, and felt his fingers tighten around her own.

'Not yet.' His voice was thick and unsteady. 'This time there's going to be no misunderstanding, Sara. This time there'll be no room in your mind for anyone but me. You've thrown your precious Rick in my face once too often, and I intend to make sure that you won't be able to spend any more nights bringing him back to life in your imagination. From now on, whenever you try to imagine he's making love to you, you are going to have the reality of my lovemaking to compete with.' His voice had become harsh again, and she was sorely tempted to tell him the truth. Instead she said pettishly, 'Jonas, I'm tired . . .' and wished she hadn't as she saw the glitter in his eyes and heard him say silkily,

'Oh, no, you're not, but you will be, I promise you that.'

And then as she closed her eyes against that glittering look she felt his mouth moving delicately against her skin, caressing the slight swell of her stomach.

Shocked by the ripple of sensation coiling through her, she struggled to move away, kicking out at him.

His fingers curled round her ankle, constraining her, and then, like the movements in some perfectly choreographed ballet, his fingertips and mouth moving in perfect synchronisation, they travelled slowly together from opposing directions to the swollen heart of her body where her womanhood awaited the gentle caress of his fingers and the sensual stroke of his tongue against and into her honeyed warmth with eager anticipation even while her mind and her conscience screamed out in shocked rejection of what he was doing to her.

She tried to squirm away from him, to deny the slow-building waves of pleasure gathering inside her, but somewhere her will deserted her and instead she heard herself crying out his name in husky supplication until he gently released her, taking her into his arms and letting her feel how much caressing her had aroused him.

'You've told me how much you want me, Sara,' he muttered thickly against her mouth. 'Now show me.'

And as though she had spent all her life in preparation for this very moment, Sara lifted herself against him, stroking her hands down his back, pressing her open lips against his throat and nuzzling his skin until she heard him groan in pleasure.

Beneath her palms his buttocks felt hard and lean. She arched up against him, her hands trembling as they sought his hips. Moving to accommodate her, he shuddered violently the first time she touched him intimately, his responsiveness to her touch unlocking some primitive force within her that wouldn't let her rest until she had guided and absorbed his body within her own.

'Love me, Jonas. Please love me.'

She was barely aware of moaning the words against his skin, or of repeating them over and over again until he silenced them with his mouth, his body re-establishing its mastery over her own as it set the pace for their lovemaking. He took her to a climax that made her cry out in astonishment and pleasure, her lips whispering his name over and over again until the sound was drowned out by his harsh cry of release, the heat of him deep within her so unbearably poignant that for a moment she felt she wanted to cry.

CHAPTER NINE

WHERE on earth was she? The angle of the light coming across the bed was unfamiliar, and so was the curious lethargy that filled her body. And then, shatteringly, she remembered. Sitting up with a cry, Sara snatched up the bedclothes as she remembered that she was naked, but she needn't have bothered; she was completely alone.

Hardly daring to believe the previous night had actually happened, she glanced fearfully at the pillow next to her own. Sure enough, it still held the indentation of another head.

Jonas. Where was he? There was no sound from the adjoining bathroom. She glanced at her watch, appalled to discover how late she had slept; Jonas must be outside working. Thank God for that. At least that meant she would be able to leave without enduring the humiliation of having to see him again. In fact, she decided as she gathered up her clothes and locked herself in the bathroom, she intended to make sure she never had to see him again. Her mind was a mass of seething feverish thought as she tried to make plans. She would tell Sam that she needed to spend some time in London looking for accommodation and a job; he would protest, but she would convince him, and Vanessa was there to take care of Carly. It wouldn't be long before he and Vanessa married. The wedding . . . She would have to attend the wedding and Jonas would be there. She winced as she put her full weight on her aching ankle; she would have to overcome that hurdle later. For now she must put as much distance between herself and Jonas as she could.

On her way through the bedroom she caught sight of her flushed face and hurriedly averted her eyes. She even looked different—more alive . . . more feminine somehow.

She was just reaching for the door handle when it turned and the door opened inwards. Confronted by the reality of the man who had been her lover, she blushed a warmer pink, all the mental images she had been trying to blot out from the moment she had woken up now surging into her mind. She almost cringed as she remembered how Jonas had made her say his name and plead for his lovemaking. In the cold light of day she ought to have been wondering how on earth it had ever happened, but even that refuge was denied to her. By admitting her real feelings towards him she was forced also to admit that if he were to touch her now, to take her in his arms . . .

But he did no such thing. Instead he folded his arms over his chest and stood in front of the door glaring at her in an uncompromising fashion while he demanded curtly, 'Just where the hell do you think you're going?'

'Home,' she told him coolly. 'Sam will be expecting me.'

'Sam will be expecting you when I drive you back after lunch.' He glanced at his watch. 'It's now only eleven o'clock. Before you leave here, you and I have some talking to do.'

Fear crawled through her. Had he guessed the truth? Was he going to confront her with it, to make her admit it as last night he had made her . . .

'Sara!' His voice was rough with anger, and something else. Compassion? She looked at him and saw the grimness of his mouth. No, she must have imagined it.

'For God's sake stop looking at me like that! I'm not going to hurt you.'

The harshness of his expression was unconvincing.

'I'd never use force against a woman.'

'No?' Somehow she managed to keep her voice light and dry. 'What about last night?' She was amazed to see the momentary heat stinging his skin. 'You forced me to . . .'

'To admit that you wanted us to make love? That wasn't the sort of force I was talking about, and you know it. Sara, for God's sake why do you fight me like this? You wanted me, I wanted you.'

'No . . . No, I didn't want you. I wanted Rick,' she lied huskily. 'I told you that last night but you wouldn't accept it, so I let you believe you were right, and I let myself believe it was Rick who held me in his arms. The fact that he and I had never actually been lovers made it easier somehow. There were no comparisons I could make. You might have possessed me physically, Jonas, but that was all it was; emotionally, mentally, in all the ways that count, it was Rick who was my lover.'

She said it fiercely, trying to convince herself as much as she tried to convince him, only she knew too much to be able to accept the lie. Jonas, obviously, did

not. All the colour drained from his face; his eyes
when they focused on her were a blank, opaque grey,
his body so tense that her throat suddenly ached with
her need to recall her cruel words. But what good
would it do?

'You were right,' said Jonas flatly, confirming all
her own private thoughts. 'It was just sex between us
after all. That's what I came up here to tell you. I
realised last night that the woman I thought you were
just doesn't exist. Still,' his mouth curled slightly, 'it
has to be admitted that it was very good sex. I've never
had a virgin before. It was quite an experience; all that
pent-up frustration. Perhaps we ought to repeat it
some time?'

His crudeness stunned her. It was the very last thing
she had expected, but she saw as she stepped past him
to walk through the door that, despite his cool voice
and rigid stance, inwardly he was ragingly angry. She
could see it in his eyes.

She had been right not to let him guess the truth, she
decided shakily as she hobbled to the top of the stairs.
He would have enjoyed tormenting her with it.

In the event, none of her plans for making sure she did
not need to see him again could be put into effect. The
day after Sara's return to the cottage, Vanessa went
down with a 'flu bug which made it impossible for her
to take charge of Carly, and in fact Sara found she was
spending a good deal of her time at Jonas's house
nursing her sister-in-law to-be.

Jonas, she noticed, kept well out of sight whenever
she was in the house, and in the third week of her

convalescence Vanessa complained that she was worried that Jonas was working far too hard.

'He's out almost from dawn to dusk,' she told Sara worriedly, 'and I know it's taking its toll on him, because he's so grim. The one thing you could always rely on Jonas for was his sense of humour, but when I started to tell him about how you almost jumped out of your skin when Peter drove the Land Rover into the yard the other day, he almost bit my head off.'

'You should be worrying about Sam now, not your brother,' Sara advised, wanting to get off such a potentially dangerous subject.

'Mmm. I do wish Jonas would settle down and get married. He needs a wife, and he'd make such a good father. He loves kids, you know. You should have seen him with Carly the other day when Sam brought her round. Do you know, that's the first time I can remember him taking any time off since I've been ill, and it would have to be the day you weren't here, too. At one time I really hoped that you and he . . . Sara . . . what on earth's wrong?' Vanessa asked worriedly, as Sara suddenly went pale and clutched on to the back of a chair for support.

She had got up quickly, unable to bear listening to Vanessa talking about Jonas any longer, and had suddenly felt dreadfully faint.

'It's nothing. I'm fine now,' she assured Vanessa as she sat down.

'Oh, I hope you're not going to go down with this 'flu, not with the wedding only a month away.'

Sara smile wanly; she was pretty sure she wasn't starting with 'flu. For the past four mornings in succession she had been quite sick on waking, and she was well enough acquainted with her own system to suspect she had met that fate at one time supposed to be the worst possible one that could befall an unmarried woman. If she was pregnant there was no way she could have the baby. How could she? She had no home, no job . . . The complications arising if she continued with the pregnancy were so potentially convoluted and damaging. Jonas was going to be Sam's brother-in-law; how on earth could she have his illegitimate child?

These were the logical and reasoned arguments she kept well to the forefront of her mind the next day as she drove into Dorchester. In her handbag was a piece of paper bearing the name and address of a charitable organisation that counselled girls in her position and, if necessary, helped them to arrange a termination. Termination? She shivered tensely, knowing that not even in her own thoughts did she want to admit what she was doing. She was going to arrange for her baby to be aborted, its short life ended almost before it had begun.

Nausea clawed at the pit of her stomach as she tried to stem the flood-tide of her thoughts. Her heart revolted against the idea, but she was trying not to listen to her heart. She had spent all last night, all the last few nights, in fact, telling herself that she mustn't be emotional and illogical, that she must bear in mind that her decision wouldn't just affect herself, that she could hardly go away and have her baby in complete secrecy like a heroine in a novelette. Sam would have to know, and being Sam he would want to hear the name of the father. And, knowing her, he would also know that she had not taken him as a lover light-heartedly. No ... No, termination was the only way.

But when she had parked the car, she found her footsteps dragging as she made her way to the small, cluttered office belonging to the organisation. Oh God, she thought, I *can't* ...

The counsellor who saw her was brisk but under-standing, not attempting to put pressure on her in any way, but competently outlining the alternatives to her. There were questions Sara had to answer, notes that had to be made, and even when she managed to anounce her decision without wavering, the counsellor suggested firmly, 'We normally advise people to take two or three days to think over their decison; after all, at this stage it is still reversible ... You wouldn't believe the number of girls who find that once the immediate anxiety of doing something about their pregnancy has gone, they have second thoughts. I can't tell you the number of girls we get coming in here to show off their babies—girls who originally were most adamant that they wanted an abortion.'

Forcing her mouth to curl into a polite smile, Sara left.

The street in which the office was housed was a long, busy one cluttered with shoppers on a Thursday afternoon, but Sara reached the end of it without realising how she had done so. Somehow she found her way back to her car and drove home to the cottage.

Mercifully it was empty. Vanessa, she learned later, had taken Sam and Carly to Essex to introduce them to her mother and Jonas's father.

They came back late, so full of high spirits and chatter that none of them noticed how withdrawn she was.

The discovery of her pregnancy caused a delay in her plans to find herself a flat and a job in London just as soon as she could, and just over a week after her initial interview with her counsellor, as she stood shakily in her bathroom, still slightly weak from the effect of her morning sickness, Sara reflected that it was just as well that Sam's bedroom was downstairs. If it hadn't been for that, there was no way she could have kept her condition a secret from her brother. As it was, he had started worrying about her pallor and lack of appetite, and she had also noticed that he had taken to watching her covertly. She had practically made up her mind what she was going to do. Two days ago she had had another meeting with her counsellor who, after talking with her, had quietly made an appointment for her at a small private clinic. She was to attend there this morning, and because her pregnancy was still at a relatively non-advanced stage there would be no necessity for her to stay overnight. Deliberately Sara had forced herself to ignore what was happening. She told herself she must pretend it was all part of some horrible nightmare; that was the only way she could endure what she had to do. Even now, her hand hovered protectively over her stomach, her heart revolting against her decision. But what real alternative did she have?

She had told Sam she was going into Dorchester to do some shopping. Now, when she went downstairs to tell him she was about to leave, he frowned at her, catching hold of her wrist and tugging her towards him when she would have turned away.

'You don't look well, Sara,' he said gently. 'Something's wrong. What is it? Surely you can tell me? Is it because Vanessa and I are getting married? Because you think I'm betraying Holly's memory?'

He saw the answer in her eyes even before she shook her head vigorously. Admitting her love for Jonas had forced her to admit other things she had been reluctant to see. Sam had been right when he said that Holly would not have wanted him and Carly to mourn her for the rest of their lives.

'It's Jonas, isn't it?' he said quietly. 'No, don't deny it, Sara.'

'You haven't said . . .'

'I haven't said a word to anyone,' he reassured her firmly. 'And nor will I do so. Is it because of him that you want to leave and go back to London? Why? He seemed attracted to you.'

'Attraction isn't love,' she broke in hastily. It was too painful to talk to Sam like this. Listening to him brought home to her how impossible it was for her to continue with her pregnancy. If she did, there was no way Sam would not immediately guess the identity of the baby's father. If the situation wasn't so tragic it might almost be farcical; put them in period costumes and they could all be actors in one of Congreve's witty plays on morals and manners.

'Strange how things work out,' Sam mused. 'You came down here determined to believe Jonas the villain of the piece, the cruel landowner intent on hounding Miss Betts; you were convinced that you'd never love anyone but Rick, and . . .'

'And I've been proved wrong on both counts. Far from hounding Miss Betts, Jonas was actually very kind to her. I know that, Sam, and I also know I was wrong about Rick. My love for him was a young girl's love, while Jonas . . . I can't talk about it,' she told him painfully. 'I have to go out; I . . .'

'Don't run away from your feelings, Sara,' Sam cautioned her gently. 'You know, you could be wrong. Jonas . . .'

'Jonas doesn't love me,' she interrupted, trying to stop her mouth from trembling as, with a sense of well and truly having burnt her boats behind her, she added huskily, 'physically he might want me, Sam, but that's all there is to it. I know because he told me so himself.'

She couldn't bear to see the pity she knew would be in her brother's eyes, and, tugging her wrist free of his grip, she hurried out to her car.

She was in no state to drive, but luckily she had the country road almost entirely to herself until she got nearer to Dorchester. The clinic was housed in a new building, recently constructed but designed to fit in with the architecture of the rest of the town. She had to park five minutes' walk away from it, but as she drew closer to the building she found her footsteps dragging. Outside she delayed even longer, fumbling in her handbag for her appointment card and holding it in her hand while she took a deep steadying breath. What on earth was she delaying for? Her decision had already been made; there was, after all, no other choice. Surely her talk with Sam only this morning had confirmed that? And yet still she hesitated, drawing a curious stare from a couple of nurses who emerged from the building. A cold sweat gripped her body; beads of perspiration lined her forehead, and her palms were clammy and chilled. She wanted to walk up the steps, but somehow her legs wouldn't obey her, and then suddenly, as she stared at the closed door, Sara knew that she couldn't go through with it.

The relief that followed the admission made her feel as giddy as though she had drunk a full glass of wine. She felt like laughing and crying at the same time, and so shaky that it was several seconds before she could turn away from the clinic and walk down the street.

The appointment card still clutched tightly in her hand, she wasn't even aware that she was crying until her surroundings became so blurred that she realised something was wrong.

She put a shaking hand up to her face, unaware of the curious stares of passers-by as she looked unseeingly at her damp fingers. Someone jostled her as they hurried past, and she collided abruptly with a lamp-post.

'Sara!'

The shock of hearing her name spoken by the last man on earth she wanted to see, the hard warmth of his fingers on her arm as he steadied her, had the opposite effect from that intended.

The world swung wildly out of focus as Jonas moved closer to her, shielding her from the buffeting bodies and curious eyes, a harshly grim look about his mouth as he said her name again.

But she was beyond hearing it, beyond doing

anything other than sinking gratefully into the darkness waiting for her.

When she came round she was lying down in the back of Jonas's car. He was leaning against the open door, watching her grimly. In his hand ... her eyes darted helplessly back to his face as she saw the small, betraying appointment card.

'It was mine, wasn't it?' he demanded harshly. 'My child and you ...'

Something in her face must have given her away, because he suddenly tensed and then drew in a rasping breath with an effort that made his shirt stretch across his chest. Leaning into the car he placed his hand on her stomach, and said thickly, 'You haven't done it yet, have you ... Have you?'

She shook her head, the tears clogging her throat, making it almost impossible for her to do more than say in a choked whisper, 'I couldn't ... I meant to, but I couldn't go through with it,' and then she was crying in earnest, terrible, racking sobs that tore at her body.

Something in his face seemed to relax a little, although his voice was still harsh as he said, 'No, and you're not going to; I intend to make damn sure of that.'

'But I can't have it ...' She was beyond reason now, the effect of shock upon shock such that she could barely comprehend that it was actually Jonas she was talking to and not some figment of her imagination sent to play Devil's advocate. 'Even if I go away I can't keep it a secret. Sam will want to know who the father is. I couldn't lie to him, and anyway he would probably guess. How could I have your child, when Sam's marrying your sister, and . . .'

'Quite easily,' Jonas told her curtly, interrupting her muddled flow of words. 'We'll get married.'

It stemmed her tears and made her struggle to sit up so that she could look at him.

'But we can't!'

'Why not? Because you're still in love with your precious Rick?' His mouth twisted. 'Maybe, but you're carrying *my* child. A child I don't intend to let you abort, and that if you're honest you don't want to abort, otherwise you wouldn't be here now.'

It was so true that she could think of no response other than to bite painfully on her lower lip.

'But you don't want to marry me,' she said at last.

He shrugged, 'Maybe not, but I'd prefer marrying you to standing by while you destroy our child, and I agree with you. In the circumstances it isn't on that you could bring it up alone. Even if that was what I wanted, and it isn't. I've always believed that both parents are equally responsible for the conception of a child, and so are equally responsible for its upbringing and care. I've no intention or desire to play the role of part-time father.'

'But we can't marry, just like that,' protested Sara weakly. Even to her own ears her protest sounded weak and almost feeble-minded, but the shock of seeing him, the total unexpectedness of his proposal, seemed to have robbed her of the ability to reason properly. With his words, with his assumption of control, he was taking from her the burden of having to worry, and it struck her as ironic that she, who had always prided herself so much on her independence,

should be so willing to let herself be dictated to. Sitting
here in the back of his car while he frowned down at
her with curt impatience was surely the least lover-like
of situations, and yet in a way she felt happier than she
could ever remember feeling in her life. She *wanted* to
marry him, she acknowledged wryly. No doubt when
she felt stronger she would regret giving in to his
coercion, and even now some shreds of common sense
and logic warned her that nothing but heartbreak
could come from the sort of marriage Jonas would
have in mind. To marry a man without having his
love, when she loved him so desperately, was surely
the deepest folly known to womankind. And yet
others had done it before her, and she would have his
child to love. Even if she hadn't loved him she would
have been grateful to him for providing her with the
opportunity to keep her baby. But if she didn't love
him it would all be so much easier, she thought
bitterly. If she didn't love him she wouldn't be so
desperately afraid of betraying herself to him, of . . .

'You can stop thinking about it,' his curt voice told
her grittily. 'There isn't a choice, Sara, and believe me
I don't intend to let you out of my sight until you're
safely married to me. I'm not going to take the risk of
you . . .'

'We can't get married just like that,' Sara protested,
ignoring the last part of his speech. 'What will Sam
and Vanessa say . . .?'

'What can they say?' he half jeered. 'Especially
when they find out about the baby. Okay, so they
might be surprised, but they're hardly going to be
shocked.'

'It isn't that. I'm not concerned about them knowing about the baby. At least . . .' She bit her lip and looked away from him. 'If Sam thinks I'm marrying you because I'm pregnant . . .'

She was unprepared for the look of anger that flashed across his face.

'He won't know, because you're not going to say one word that will give him that impression,' he told her bitingly. 'As far as Vanessa and Sam are concerned, we're quite desperately in love with one another, and I'm so frightened of losing you that I intend to marry you just as soon as it can be arranged. In fact, I don't think we'll bother telling them; we'll just present them with a *fait accompli*.'

There were a hundred protests she ought to have made, but somehow they all remained unvoiced. It was rather shocking to discover how much she had changed, how much she craved the security and protection that Jonas gave her. Somehow it was easier to give in and let him take control than it was to protest.

'I'd like to chain you to my side from now until we get married,' he told her after they had visited the registrar and fixed up the details of the wedding, 'but since that's impossible I'm going to ask you to give me your word . . .'

'That I won't destroy your child?' she finished shakily for him. It was unnerving to realise how jealous she felt already of her unborn child, secure in its father's love in a way that she never could be. 'I want to keep my baby, Jonas,' she told him fiercely, 'and because of that . . .'

'You'll marry me. I'm not under any illusions that you'd marry me for any other reason,' he interrupted sardonically. 'But if the baby turns out to be a boy, I promise you one thing; he isn't going to be called Rick.'

Sara turned away, not wanting him to see the pain in her eyes.

Having insisted that she was in no fit condition to drive herself home, Jonas bundled her into his car, silencing her protests by saying that he would get his garage to pick hers up and drive it back for her later in the day.

Outside the cottage he cautioned her abruptly when she would have opened the door and left him the moment he stopped his car.

'Remember, by the end of the week we'll be married. If you want to convince Sam and Vanessa that it's a love match you'll have to do your bit too. I'll come in with you.'

'But my car. Sam . . .'

'We'll tell him you've got engine trouble and that having bumped into you in town I offered to bring you home. I also think we should have dinner together tonight. Oh, it's all right,' he assured her sardonically, seeing her face, 'I won't inflict my presence on you for any longer than necessary. We can eat at the house. I've got some paperwork to do, so I suggest you bring a book with you or something else to occupy your time. If we're going to be at all convincing about this marriage we have to create at least an illusion of intimacy.'

She knew that he was right, but that didn't make it

any easier to endure the sensation of his fingers against her skin as they walked towards the cottage with his arm draped casually across her shoulder.

She could see the questioning surprise in Sam's eyes when they walked in, as well she might, she thought wryly, remembering their earlier conversation.

Even so, Sam managed to hide his surprise as he chatted easily to Jonas, although he did glance rather curiously at Sara's purposefully averted face when Jonas anounced that they were having dinner together.

Sam wasn't given an opportunity to question her. Almost as though he did, in reality, not intend to let her out of his sight, Jonas insisted on taking her back to the house with him, claiming that in view of Vanessa's defection to Sam, he needed Sara's help in watering the plants in the greenhouses.

There was nothing she could do to protest effectively. There was no excuse she could give for not going with him.

They were married less than a week later. That neither Sam nor Vanessa evinced the shock she had expected was a little unnerving, and Sara was thankful that Jonas did not share her awareness of the reason behind the amused and knowledgeable smile with which Sam greeted his announcement.

They had gone straight from the register office to the cottage, and Sara now sat in silence as she listened to Jonas explaining that, because of pressure of business, they were not going to be able to go on honeymoon.

'Why on earth was there all the rush, then?' Vanessa

demanded, grimacing faintly at her stepbrother. 'Poor Sara, she didn't even have time to look for a wedding dress, not to mention what the parents will say.'

'They already know. I rang them the day Sara accepted my proposal and told them. As to the rush—well, apart from the obvious reason,' he gave Sara a long, contemplative look that made her skin colour and Vanessa exclaim, 'For heaven's sake, Jonas, you're embarrassing Sara to death, not to mention what you're doing to me!'

'And me,' Sam interrupted with a grin. 'Suddenly a whole fortnight seems far too long to wait to get you all to myself, Van,' he teased his bride-to-be.

'There is another reason.'

The seriousness of his tone alerted Sara to what he intended to do. In a fever of panic she reached out towards him, but he simply captured her hand in his, caressing the backs of her fingers in an almost absent-minded way.

'Sara is carrying my child.' Before anyone could make any comment he went on calmly, 'We had intended to wait to make our announcement until after your wedding, but in the circumstances . . .' He let his voice trail away and then turned to Sara, lifting her fingers to his mouth and lightly kissing them. Her response was totally out of proportion to the brevity of his caress. 'We both decided it was better to be completely open about the situation. After all, you'd know soon enough anyway, and I must admit I can't pretend to be anything other than delighted at the thought of becoming a father.'

Of course Sam insisted that they must all have a

drink, and it was some time before Jonas exclaimed that they would have to leave. Sara had already packed a suitcase in anticipation, and when she came downstairs with it she found Sam waiting for her at the bottom of the stairs.

'Jonas has gone with Vanessa to pick Carly up from playschool,' he announced. 'They won't be very long. How long have you known you were pregnant?' he asked quietly.

Sara's silence betrayed her.

'You didn't have to marry him, you know, Sara; you could have come to me.'

'I love him,' she responded truthfully. 'And this is the only way I could keep the baby.'

She saw Sam's face and said huskily, 'Yes, I know what you're thinking, Sam, but how could I have told you? The first thing you'd have asked me would have been the name of the father. Can't you see how embarrassing it would have been? Me pregnant by your brother-in-law. I was going to have an abortion,' she added, feeling that having told him so much he might as well hear the rest. 'I couldn't go through with it in the end, and when Jonas found out and insisted we get married it seemed the right thing to do. Oddly enough, loving him made it that much harder.'

'Does he know how you feel?'

She shook her head. 'No . . . nor will he do. Like I said before, he doesn't love me, he just . . .' She broke off as she heard the car. 'Please don't repeat any of this to Vanessa, Sam,' she begged her brother. 'I didn't want you to know, and there's no reason . . .'

'No, I won't tell her. You didn't expect him to say

anything to us about the baby, did you?'

Sara shook her head.

'Well, we would have had to know sooner or later, he was right about that, and if you hadn't told me how you felt beforehand, after his performance today I'd have been totally convinced that the pair of you were deeply in love. Are you sure that . . .'

He broke off as Sara shook her head desperately. Vanessa, Carly and Jonas were already coming up the path towards them, and Sam, correctly interpreting her gesture, adroitly changed the subject before they were close enough to hear.

Sara's initial relief that she wasn't going to be called upon to endure the torment of a honeymoon alone with Jonas was abruptly terminated when they reached the house and he coolly announced that he would take her case up to his room. 'Forgive me, I should have said *our* room,' he amended wryly.

Sara couldn't move. She stood at the bottom of the stairs too shocked to edit her thoughts as she blurted out, 'Do you mean we'll be sharing a bedroom?'

One dark eyebrow lifted satirically. 'It is the custom, and bearing in mind the fact that we're supposed to be wildly in love, Vanessa would be rather surprised, to say the least, if we deviated from it. Of course I suppose we could always improvise—suggest to her that we enjoy the romantic folly of creeping secretly from bedroom to bedroom in the small hours of the night,' he added with fine sarcasm.

'All right, you've made your point. But I don't want to share a room with you.'

'No . . . I can see that,' he agreed suavely, and then mocked dulcetly, 'as I remember it, you said you didn't want to make love with me either . . .'

'You know the reason for that.' She was so frantic that he might guess the truth that her voice was unusually sharp with tension. 'I told you, I pretended you were Rick.'

'Good heavens, not quarrelling already, are you?'

Neither of them had heard Vanessa come in, and she laughed at their expressions. 'It's all right; I'm not staying. Sam has suggested that I use your room tonight, Sara, so that you can have a token honeymoon at least. I've just come back to collect a few things. Are you taking her somewhere special tonight, Jonas?'

He recovered far faster than she could, smiling at his sister with a lazy mockery that made shivers of unwanted pleasure curl down Sara's spine.

'Yes,' he agreed softly. 'In fact I was just taking her there when you interrupted.'

Vanessa's eyes widened and then she laughed. 'I'm not sure which of us it is you're trying to shock, me or Sara,' she complained, her eyes drawn from Sara's flushed face to the flight of stairs leading up to the bedrooms. 'Take her into the drawing-room and give her a glass of champagne instead,' she suggested with a grin. 'I promise I'll be gone in ten minutes.'

In fact it was fifteen minutes before Sara heard Vanessa's small car drive away, and for every one of them she had sat in a grimly tense silence, refusing the drink Jonas offered and hating him more than she had ever thought it possible to hate a man she also loved.

She waited until the car had disappeared before

attempting to speak her anger, which was so intense that she could barely get the words out.

'How dare you humiliate me like that?' she demanded bitterly. 'How could you humiliate me in front of Vanessa by intimating . . .'

'That I couldn't wait to take you to bed?'

He was watching her face like a cat at a mousehole, she saw, and she was fearfully conscious that the room was filled with an anger that didn't emanate only from her.

'Since when has that been humiliation?' he demanded bitingly. 'Most brides would consider it perfectly normal, not to say flattering, that their new husbands were so eager to make love to them, but since we're talking of humiliation, I could point out to you that I find it less than pleasant to be constantly reminded that in your eyes my child was fathered by a ghost. You're very quick to tell me you won't share my bed, Sara, but as I remember it you didn't need much persuasion the last time.'

What he said was all too sickeningly true, and Sara blenched at what he must think of her. In his eyes she must figure no better than a cheat and a fraud, a woman who claimed to love another man, but who was willing to accept his embraces instead.

'I'm tired, Jonas,' she protested huskily and not untruthfully, unwilling to pursue her own thoughts to their conclusion and suddenly exhausted by the antipathy between them that kept her nerves in such a constant state of tension.

'You look it,' he replied. 'I'll take you upstairs and show you the room, then I'm afraid I'll have to leave you for a while.' The look he gave her was mockingly derisory. 'The greenhouses will need watering.' He glanced at his watch as he opened the door for her to precede him, and even that simple economic movement, that brief glimpse of tanned sinewy skin, was enough to make her pulses hammer.

His bedroom was larger than the one she had occupied during her overnight stay, its décor in keeping with the elegance of the room, the furniture antique and the colour scheme quite obviously chosen to blend in with the lovely faded Aubusson carpet on the floor. The bed was huge and very high, complete with solid mahogany top and tail boards. In a smaller room it would have looked ridiculous, but in here it looked exactly right.

The sheets were linen and monogrammed. Sara touched them reverently. 'They belonged to my great-grandmother,' Jonas told her. 'They were part of her trousseau, apparently. I got Mrs Lyons to make up the bed with them this morning. They seemed rather more bridal than the easy-care ones Vanessa seems to favour.'

For some reason his words hurt—perhaps because they brought home to her all that she would never have. In that one brief action she had seen an agonising glimpse of the lover Jonas would be if he really was in love. She had had another the day he had tried to tell her what he was beginning to feel for her, but she had recklessly destroyed those feelings like a small child destroying a longed-for toy in a fit of rebellious pique, and now it was too late. She shivered, and instantly he frowned.

'You're cold. Go downstairs and I'll light the fire in the sitting-room before I go out. Mrs Lyons has left us something to eat . . .'

Like a wooden doll, Sara let him guide her back downstairs. She had entered this marriage willingly; she could hardly complain now because Jonas didn't love her.

CHAPTER TEN

AFTER the first week of their marriage, Sara told herself that she had lived through the worst and she could scarcely get any more unhappy. She had learned painfully what it was like to sleep in the same bed as a man who seemed completely unaware of her presence—and equally undesirous of it, while she . . . For the first couple of nights she told herself her restlessness came from the fact that she was not used to sharing a bed with someone else, but by the end of the week she knew she was wrong. The reason she was sleeping so badly, the reason she kept on waking through the night, was that part of her still hoped that one time she would wake and find herself in Jonas's arms.

Why on earth even one part of her should be under such an illusion Sara had no idea. Since their marriage, Jonas had made it more than plain that he did not want her.

Now they had been married for two weeks, and today Vanessa and Sam were to be married.

Jonas's father and Vanessa's mother were both to attend the ceremony, and then they were all coming back here to the house for a celebratory meal. Sara had spent the past few days carefully checking with Mrs Lyons that everything would go well. Jonas was someone she had barely seen; he was up early in the morning and in late at night—often after she was in bed and asleep. Her pregnancy was making her feel very tired, although as yet it did not show.

She had bought a new outfit for the wedding. A peach-coloured suit in a slub-effect straw silk. The skirt, although straight, was a size larger than she normally wore and slightly tucked at the waist, which meant it discreetly concealed the very small swell of her stomach. It had a matching sleeveless top, but it was the jacket that had caught Sara's eye.

Loosely styled, it had long batwing sleeves ending in tight cuffs. The shoulders were cleverly padded, the jacket falling from stitched-down pleats in an attractive unstructured fashion, the bottom slightly curved like a man's shirt-tail. She had found a hat in a deeper shade of peach edged with white, which luckily meant that she could use her existing white shoes and handbag.

The wedding was to take place in the small local church. Jonas was going to be Sam's best man, while Vanessa, purely to please Carly, had decided to have the little girl as her one bridesmaid.

Sara was just putting the finishing touches to her appearance when she heard a car draw up outside. Jonas was already over at the cottage. Because of the circumstances, he was to drive both Sam and Carly to the church, while she would take Vanessa.

She looked out of the window and saw an unfamiliar car.

'The parents,' Vanessa breathed behind her. 'Bang on time. That will be Ma, of course. Oliver is hopeless about time.' She gave a small chuckle. 'Come on, we'd better go and let them in.'

For a bride-to-be, Vanessa was amazingly calm, much calmer than Sara herself had been, but then Vanessa was marrying a man who she knew beyond any doubt loved her, Sara acknowledged miserably.

She had been dreading meeting Jonas's parents, feeling sure that they must think that her pregnancy had forced Jonas into marrying her.

But if those were their feelings they certainly didn't betray them when Vanessa opened the door to them and urged them inside.

Oliver Chesney was amazingly like his son; older of course, and rather stooped, his hair silver and not black. His eyes weren't like Jonas's. They were a faded blue, and very kind, if somewhat vague. He acknowledged Vanessa with a smile and shook hands warmly with Sara—she was to learn later that he was not a demonstrative man—and then almost straight away started to comment on the ducks he had noticed swimming on the village pond.

'Unusual that, to see them here at this time off year. They should be in Iceland. Of course, we did have some bad spring gales which could have blown them of course.'

'Oliver, we've come to see Vanessa getting married, not birdwatch,' his wife reminded him with patient firmness.

'Of course. Of course . . .' The blue eyes focused and he smiled charmingly at Sara. 'Forgive me, Sara, I do tend to get rather carried away with my hobby at times, I'm afraid, as Vanessa already knows.'

'Too true,' groaned Vanessa ruefully. 'While all my

schoolfriends were holidaying in Spain and Greece, we were chasing off after birds or plants, invariably somewhere cold and wet.'

'You're exaggerating, darling,' her mother protested. 'What about that lovely holiday we had in Switzerland?'

'You mean the one when Oliver got stuck half-way up a mountain trying to photograph a rare flower?'

Her mother laughed, and then turned to Sara. 'We're being very rude, reminiscing like this, Sara. I'm sorry we couldn't make it to your wedding, but Oliver was just putting the final touches to his latest book, and his publishers were screaming out for it.'

Vanessa had already told her that in retirement Jonas's father had turned to writing about his favourite subjects, and had already had two books published.

'What time are we due at the church?' Jennifer Chesney asked, automatically taking charge.

When Vanessa told her, she said calmly, 'Good, that leaves us time to have a cup of coffee. No, Oliver, you are not to go out and lose yourself in the garden,' she checked her husband, seeing him wandering in the direction of the French window. 'Vanessa, you go and make us all a drink while I get acquainted with my new daughter-in-law.'

'We weren't totally surprised by Jonas's news,' she announced. 'Vanessa had already told us about you, and hinted that Jonas was showing a far more than neighbourly interest in you. I must say that I'm delighted that he's finally fallen in love and married. Both of us have been worried about him for some time,' she added, glancing affectionately across at her husband who was still looking wistfully out into the garden. 'As Oliver would be the first one to admit, he isn't the best person in the world at personal relationships. He was brought up by a bachelor uncle and went through the traditional public school system, so when Jonas's mother died, poor Oliver didn't really have the faintest idea of how to comfort or bring up his son.

'Jonas was at a particularly vulnerable age when he lost his mother, and naturally he wasn't able to turn to me. I was the intruder who had taken his mother's place. We've talked about it since, and he says that the hardest thing was not coming to terms with the fact that his father had found a second wife, but that he himself actually liked me. He said that made him feel doubly guilty, as though he were in some way betraying the memory of his mother. Those are very strong emotions for a boy of fourteen to try to handle, and although everything has resolved itself now, they have left scars. I've noticed how very withdrawn he's always been with his girl-friends—and there have been plenty of them,' she added drily. 'He's a very attractive man, but I could sense that he was always holding something back, and I must confess I'd begun to worry that he'd never let himself fall in love.'

As Vanessa came in with the coffee, Jennifer Chesney changed the subject to ask her daughter about her wedding dress, and Sara tactfully suggested that she stay and keep her father-in-law company while Jennifer went upstairs to help Vanessa get ready.

The silence that fell after they had gone was not an uncomfortable one. In fact, Oliver Chesney was one of the most restful and placid people Sara had ever been with. He had a sweet naïveté about him that Sara couldn't help contrasting with Jonas's far harder exterior.

And yet Jonas had known pain and loss, just as she had herself. Had, if she was to believe Jennifer, experienced feelings about his relationship with his stepmother that were very close to her own emotional turmoil when she intially met him.

Surely, in the circumstances, he would understand if she tried to explain to him exactly why she had so determinedly clung to her memories of Rick? But why should she explain? What was the point?

The point was that within a very short space of time she and Jonas would be the parents of a child—a child who had a right to expect love and security from them. The love she sensed their child already had—from Jonas as well as herself—but the security? Being honest with Jonas would not change his lack of love for her, but surely it might at least open the way to a better understanding between them? To a relationship at least founded on something more solid than their present precariously vulnerable foundations.

But did she have the courage to do it? Could she actually find the words to admit to him that she had clung so desperately to the protection of Rick because she had been frightened by her response to him; that she had hated and resented him because paradoxically she had known even then how much she could love him?

She must tell him, Sara decided an hour later as she set her car in motion. She would have to wait until after the wedding now, but once it was over and they were alone . . . Now that the decision had been made, she felt curiously better, as though a terrible burden had slid from her shoulders.

Vanessa had chosen a very simple wedding dress, but one which suited her slender figure perfectly. The way Sam looked at his bride as they left the church together made Sara's throat ache with suppressed longing for Jonas to look at her with such tender love. What a foolish, impossible dream, she recognised a little later as she studied his cool, slightly forbidding features. Today he seemed to have retreated even further away from her than ever.

The meal after the wedding was a very evident success. Sara watched Jonas and his father chatting with a tiny ache in her heart. They got on very well together, and she couldn't help wondering how Jonas would react to his own child. They hadn't even discussed the baby since their marriage. In fact they hadn't even discussed anything at all. Did Jonas now resent the fact that he had married her? It had, after all, been by his own choice.

Because she was carrying his child, because he was the sort of man who took his responsibilities seriously. A man who would show the degree of concern for an old woman who was no relative that he had shown for Miss Betts would never be able to turn his back on his own child.

Now, when it was too late, Sara wondered if she had let Jonas persuade her into marriage too easily, but if she had refused . . .

'Are you feeling all right?'

Lost in her own unhappy thoughts, she hadn't seen him come over to her. The light pressure of his hand on her shoulder and the concern in his voice both combined to bring her perilously close to tears.

'Just a bit tired,' she told him, not untruthfully. It was bliss—heaven, in fact—to be the recipient of his concern.

'Why don't you go upstairs and rest for a while?' he suggested. 'Everyone will be leaving pretty soon.'

Nodding her head, Sara made her excuses to everyone and went upstairs. Undressing down to her underwear, she lay on the bed, drifting in and out of a restless sleep, finally waking when she heard goodbyes being called and car doors slamming.

Several minutes later Jonas came upstairs.

'I'll have to go and check up on the greenhouses shortly, but I'd thought I'd come up and see if you wanted a cup of tea or anything first.'

Sara shook her head. Her throat felt dry, and she was as tense as a finely coiled spring, but she might never get an opportunity like this again.

'I don't want anything to drink, Jonas,' she told him huskily, 'but I would like to talk to you.'

He approached the bed warily, sitting down on the edge of it, almost as far away from her as he could possibly get, she noticed wryly.

Slowly, haltingly, she started to explain to him the trauma of her inner battle against herself almost from the moment they met.

He listened to her in silence, his face grave and

unreadable, and then said emotionlessly, 'I can understand what you're saying, Sara—I went through much the same thing when my father remarried—but what I don't understand is how any of this relates to me. I already knew how you felt about Rick. I knew you couldn't bear the thought of putting someone else in his place . . .'

He had missed the point completely, or perhaps she hadn't put it clearly enough, Sara thought desperately, anxiety making her tongue clumsy and her throat tight as she shook her head and said frantically, 'No . . . no, you don't understand. What I'm trying to tell you, Jonas, is that I love you.'

Instantly his face became a mask of rejection. He got up and walked over to the window, standing with his back to her. An icy wave of humiliation overwhelmed her as Sara stared at his tensed back.

'What is it exactly that you hope to achieve by telling me this now, Sara?' He had turned to face her, his face hard, his eyes a cold implacable grey. 'Oh, I can guess,' he suggested softly. 'Sexual frustration plays the very devil with one's principles, doesn't it?' He stood watching her with his hands in his pockets, his stance relaxed and yet at the same time curiously tense and watchful. 'There was no need to go to these lengths, you know,' he mocked her. 'A simple and far more direct request for physical satisfaction would have done equally well. In fact, I thought we'd already agreed that sex was all there was or could be between us.'

His words were like blows, beating her to the ground, causing her such unimaginable pain that she couldn't stay and endure them. She had to escape.

She got off the bed and ran to the door, but before she reached it she tripped on a tuck in the Aubusson carpet. As she lost her balance she saw a blur as Jonas moved, but it was too late and she heard herself cry out as she caught the side of her head on the edge of the door.

The smell struck her first, vaguely familiar and for some reason very frightening. The smell was associated with something she wanted to escape from, something she had to prevent. She tried to move and found that she was somehow constrained. Someone was holding her down, or so it seemed. Panic built up inside her and she knew what it was she feared. The smell she recognised was clinical and clean—a hospital smell. She wanted to cry out that she had changed her mind, that she wanted to keep her baby, but somehow the words wouldn't form. She struggled to open her eyes and then closed them quickly as the sharp brightness struck them.

'It's all right, Mrs Chesney. You're perfectly safe.' A nurse was leaning over her, smiling warmly. 'You had a nasty fall, but you're all right now.'

'A fall . . . her heartbeat steadied slightly. So she hadn't come in to get rid of her baby. Her baby. Her hand touched her stomach protectively. A fall, the nurse had said. Suddenly it all came back. She lifted her aching head off the pillow to call out to the nurse, but she had gone.

She was in a private room, Sara recognised, staring at the massed flowers and the television set.

The door opened and she looked up eagerly, anticipating the return of the nurse, but it wasn't she who stood there, it was Jonas.

He looked grey and ill, a different man almost, and fear clutched at her again. She tried to sit up, but the effort was too much for her.

'My baby?'

How weak and hesitant her voice sounded, when she felt as though she had all but screamed the words at him!

Watching Jonas, Sara saw his expression lighten immediately and knew that whatever it was that had brought that drawn quality to his face, it had not been a miscarriage.

'He or she is fine,' he told her with a small smile. 'In fact you're both fine, luckily. Dr Heathers was very worried when you first came in—that was some crack you gave your head—but apart from mild concussion it seems you're OK. You'll have a nasty collection of bruises for a while, and possibly even a black eye.'

'I thought when I woke up that I'd come in for the abortion.' Sara spoke slowly, saying the words more for her own benefit than for his. 'I wanted to tell them that I'd changed my mind, but I couldn't speak.' She shivered, her eyes unknowingly agonised. 'It was terrible . . . awful . . .'

She was stunned when Jonas came across to the bed and sat on the edge of it, facing her, taking her in his arms.

He was wearing one of his soft woollen checked shirts, and the fabric felt good against her face. Through it she could smell his skin and she wanted to

bury her head against him and go on breathing in the
essence of him for the rest of her life. She could feel his
heartbeat, surely highly accelerated. One of his hands
stroked her hair. It must be a dream, she thought
hazily, and hadn't realised she had said the words out
loud until he released her rather abruptly and said
curtly, 'Doctor Heathers says you're well enough to go
home, but of course if you'd prefer to stay in for
another day or so.'

'Another day? How long have I been here?'

'Two days,' Jonas told her. He had his back to her
and his voice was muffled. The words sounded almost
anguished, that could not possibly be—witness the
way he had released her so quickly just now.

'I should never have spoken to you the way I did.'
He said it under his breath, swinging round abruptly.
The expression of anguish in his eyes shocked her. For
a moment hope, golden with promise, floated through
her, and then she was dashed back down to reality
when he went on rawly, 'You could have so easily lost
the baby, and . . .'

'And then you'd have married me for nothing,' she
supplied bitterly for him.

She watched him frown, but the anger she
anticipated wasn't there. If anything his expression
was rather abstracted as he asked her slowly, 'Why did
you tell me you loved me?'

Why? Why had she? 'I thought it might help to get
our marriage on a better footing.'

'A conciliatory lie, in other words?'

A lie? He was still watching her, and Sara felt her
heart leap and lodge in her throat. Without knowing

it, he was giving her an opportunity to retract, to pretend she had never really meant what she had said, or was he simply offering her a way out that would embarrass neither of them; was this his way of telling her that he didn't want her love, either now or at any time in the future? For a second she toyed with the idea of telling him that she hadn't lied, that she did love him, but what good would it do? With her mind growing clearer with every passing second, she could all too easily remember the anger and contempt with which he had greeted her admission of love.

Even so, she couldn't bring herself to actually tell him yet another lie. Instead she shrugged and, avoiding his eyes, said listlessly, 'If you like.'

The silence stretched on for so long that she was forced at last to look at him. He was frowning slightly, sharp grooves of pain scoring his skin. She wanted to go up to him and take him in her arms to tell him how much she loved him.

The door opened and a nurse came in.

'All ready to get dressed, are we?' she demanded brightly of Sara, starting to shoo Jonas out. 'Doctor will be in to have a few words with you before you leave.' Taking Jonas with her, she left Sara to get dressed.

Jonas seemed very preoccupied on the drive back to the house. Despite her protests, he insisted on carrying her inside the house and depositing her carefully on a settee in the sitting-room, saying that Mrs Lyons had been in and left them something to eat. 'There was a card from Vanessa and Sam this morning.'

The newly married couple and Carly were still on

honeymoon, and Sara tried to will her tensed muscles to relax as Jonas disappeared in the direction of the kitchen. He seemed different in a way she couldn't quite put her finger on; gentler somehow.

He wasn't gone long, coming back with a loaded tea-trolley. Sara stared at the mounds of sandwiches and scones.

'Mrs Lyons believes in ladies in your interesting condition eating for two,' he told her with a grin.

'There's enough there to feed two hundred!' exclaimed Sara wryly. In point of fact she wasn't hungry at all; sitting here listening to his lazy drawl, having this brief glimpse of the relationship they might have had had things been different, was suddenly far too painful. She felt as though her throat was raw with the threat of tears. Her head ached and so did her heart. When she put down her sandwich untouched, she saw Jonas frown.

'Are you feeling all right?'

He was at her side instantly, watching her, lifting his fingers to her face and touching the still tender flesh of her temple, pushing back her hair as his fingertips caressed her skin in what she could only assume must be an automatic reflex action. Whatever the origin of the caress, it was playing havoc with her self-control. She wanted him to go on; she wanted him to stop. She made a small sound of protest in her throat, her eyes meeting his for an unguarded second. Amazingly, he was smiling at her, a warm, teasing smile that held so much promise that for a moment her heart seemed to stop beating.

Dropping down beside her so that their heads were

level, he took her wrists in a light grip and said huskily, 'Sara, are you sure you were lying when you said you loved me?'

His question was so unexpected that she simply stared at him, while a betraying tide of colour swept up under her skin.

His grip on her wrists tightened; the warmth of his breath brushed against her skin as he muttered, more it seemed to himself than to her, 'Silly question.' And then his mouth was touching hers, moving against it with a heady languor that made her bones melt, clinging and caressing, moving so gradually from possession to passion that Sara was barely aware of how the transition took place.

Somewhere on the outer periphery of her mind was the fact that this time she had quite definitely burned her boats behind her; there was no way now that Jonas would ever believe she did not love him. Having come to that realisation, it seemed futile to even think of trying to resist him; it would have been impossible anyway.

She felt his fingers thread through her hair, holding her head so that she couldn't avoid the drowning ravishment of his kiss.

Shamingly, when at last he released her mouth, her lips clung protestingly to his. His tongue touched them lightly and then he was releasing her and pushing her firmly back into her seat.

Standing up, he studied her for several seconds while she cursed the hot betraying colour scorching her skin, dreading whatever he might be about to say.

It was every bit as bad as she had anticipated.

'You do love me, don't you?' he said at last.

What was the point of denying it? 'Yes. Probably almost right from the first time we met, but I didn't want to admit it. I was frightened, you see ... Frightened of loving someone again and losing them the way I lost Rick.'

'Yes, I know.'

'You must find all this quite amusing.'

Heavens, how on earth was she going to endure this? Even her voice was betraying her, shaking over the words.

'Must I?' His hands cupped her face, tilting it so that she was obliged to look at him. 'Do I look as though I'm amused?'

She looked at him, and trembled at what she saw in his eyes, unable to believe the hungry, aching way he was looking at her. Then he groaned and said her name huskily, half laughing. 'Dear God, Sara, what you've put me through!'

She was in his arms, and he was kissing her with all the passion and need she had dreamed of, pushing her blouse out of the way so that his mouth could caress her throat and shoulder. She shivered and gasped in pleasure as his hand found her breast.

'Do I feel as though I'm amused?' he demanded, pulling her hard against him so that she could feel his arousal. 'I love you, you crazy, blind idiot; I think I fell in love with you the moment I saw you! And all you could do was keep on telling me about Rick.'

He kissed her again, and she moved wantonly against him, enjoying his smothered indrawn breath.

'Enough,' he told her thickly, releasing her and

pushing her gently away. 'Explanations first, love-making later.'

'Mmm. I think I'd rather have the lovemaking first,' Sara protested happily, but she let him settle her comfortably beside him on the settee and put her head contentedly on his shoulder.

'I can't tell you what it did to me when you ran out of the bedroom like that. I tried to warn you about the carpet, but it was too late . . .' She looked up at him, catching the anguish in his voice.

'I should never have said what I did to you, but I was half out of my mind with rage and jealousy. First you tell me you don't love me and never will, then when I make love to you you tell me you were pretending I was another man. You'll never know how much that hurt me. After the way you'd responded to me in my arms, I was convinced you must feel something for me. I suspected all that talk about only loving Rick and just wanting me for sex was a protective wall you were hiding behind, but when you told me you'd pretended I was Rick, I knew it didn't matter a bit whether I thought you loved me or not, if *you* wouldn't let yourself believe it. That's why it came as such a kick in the teeth when you calmly announced that you loved me. All I could think was that you'd decided to go on playing your little game of pretending I was Rick. You couldn't ever have him, so I was the next best thing . . .'

'It wasn't like that at all,' protested Sara softly. 'Although I can follow your reasoning.'

'It was such an abrupt about-face. Right up until

our marriage you kept on saying you loved Rick, and then suddenly . . .'

'Not quite as suddenly as all that,' admitted Sara huskily. 'I knew I loved you the night we made love . . .' She saw him looking at her and added softly, 'Before we made love, in actual fact, but it was such a shock; I was so terrified you would find out how I felt . . . and so nearly demented by my own fear of loving anyone, that I lied to you and told you I'd pretended you were Rick. You see, even though you'd said to me that you were beginning to fall in love with me, I didn't want you to love me. I was frightened of loving or being loved because I felt it would only lead to pain.'

'We've both made mistakes. I tried to rush you into loving me before you were really ready. I was scared to death of losing you even then.' Jonas looked sombrely at her.

'When I realised you and Rick had never been lovers, it gave me the kind of primitive pleasure I'd always taught myself to despise. That's why I over-reacted so much when you told me you'd pretended I *was* Rick. I'd been congratulating myself because I thought you'd cared enough about me to take me as your first lover, when in reality you weren't making love with me at all—or at least that's what I thought.'

'Even before you made love to me I knew you aroused me in a way that Rick never had,' Sara said. 'And knowing that only increased my fear. I didn't *want* to feel like that about you, because . . .'

'Because you were frightened of losing me as you lost Rick,' Jonas finished softly for her. 'Life doesn't come with any guarantees, Sara, but whatever the future might hold, at least we have this now.'

'Yes.' She shivered suddenly, wondering what would have happened if she had gone through with the abortion and gone to London. When she voiced her thoughts, Jonas looked at her gravely.

'It wouldn't have altered my feelings for you,' he told her softly. 'Somehow I'd have found you, persuaded you that you couldn't live without me, although I must admit I felt the gods had finally decided to smile on me the day I found you in Dorchester. I'm sorry about the baby,' he added soberly, 'I should have been more careful, but somehow at the time . . . It hadn't occurred to me then that you and Rick had never been lovers.'

'We were rather reckless,' Sara agreed, 'but I'm not sorry to be having your child, Jonas.' She shivered with pleasure at the way he looked at her.

'You've no idea how I felt when I saw you fall. It flashed through my mind that you might lose the baby because of my cruelty, and I knew that you wanted it. I lashed out at you in a fury because you'd hurt me. I told myself you couldn't possibly mean it when you said you loved me. I thought you were lying to me. It was only later when I'd had time to calm down, when I'd spent hours sitting at your bedside and praying that you were going to be all right, that I realised that you just might possibly have meant it. You can imagine how that made me feel,' he added wryly.

'What convinced you?'

'The way you avoided looking at me when I asked you if what you'd said was true. That—and of course this,' he murmured softly, taking her in his arms and touching his mouth almost teasingly to hers.

Sara was reluctant to let him go, her eyes darkening slightly as he stood up.

'Come on.' He tugged her to her feet, the gleam in his eyes belying his cool drawl.

'Where are we going?' She was envisaging being roped into helping him with the evening watering, but then he laughed and said softly, 'Dr Heathers said it might be a good idea if you were to spend your first couple of days at home in bed. I fully intend to make sure that you do.'

'It's four o'clock in the afternoon!' Sara exclaimed, but it was only a half-hearted protest, quickly changing to a smothered sound of pleasure when he silenced it with a teasingly provocative kiss. Her arms slid round his neck, her fingers burrowing into his hair, and when he released her mouth she buried her face against him, breathing in the scent of him appreciatively.

When she opened her eyes he was looking at her with an openly fierce hunger. Her fingers curled into the open neck of his shirt, her breathing suddenly accelerating.

'Jonas!'

Her voice held all her pent-up desire and love for him, and she felt his response in the sudden tensing of his muscles. His hands cupped her face and he looked down into it as though he was memorising each individual feature, his voice raw and husky as he muttered, 'I love you more than I imagined I could ever love another human being, Sara. Finding the words to tell you how much is too difficult and time-consuming. That's why I'm going to show you instead.'

Without a word she gave him her hand and walked with him towards the stairs. She had been lucky, far more lucky than she privately felt she deserved.

At the top of the stairs Jonas paused and turned her to face him, his expression grave as he said softly, 'You know, I think if we have a son I'd like to call him Rick after all. Partially as a reminder and partially as a thank you.'

Very shakily Sara told him, 'I think I'd like that. Sam told me not so long ago that I loved Rick the way a girl does her first love, but that it wasn't a woman's love for a man. I wouldn't admit it at the time, but he was right. He also told me that Rick would never have wanted me to mourn him for the rest of my life. He was right about that as well. I'll remember him in the way that a girl always does remember her first adolescent love, and in time I think I'll even learn not to feel guilty because I never did and never could love him the way I love you.'

'Thank you.' Only the huskiness of Jonas's voice betrayed how much her words meant to him, but the touch of his fingers against her skin conveyed a need of a different kind, one that caused her to abandon all thoughts of the past and urge him with mutely imploring eyes to fulfil the promise implicit in his touch.

When he picked her up and carried her towards the bed, she knew that there would never be anyone who could mean to her what Jonas did, and as he laid her gently on the bed and leaned down to kiss her, she prayed that she would never be called upon to face life without him.

'Love me,' she murmured the words against his lips.

'I'm going to!'

It was a misunderstanding that could cost a young woman her
virtue, and a notorious rake his heart.

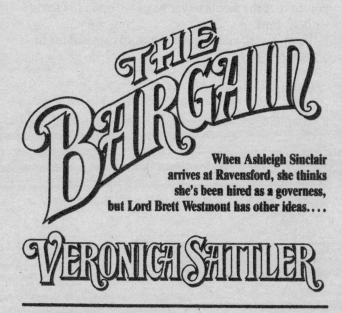

THE BARGAIN

When Ashleigh Sinclair
arrives at Ravensford, she thinks
she's been hired as a governess,
but Lord Brett Westmont has other ideas....

VERONICA SATTLER

ATTRACTIVE, SPACE SAVING BOOK RACK

Display your most prized novels on this handsome and sturdy book rack. The hand-rubbed walnut finish will blend into your library decor with quiet elegance, providing a practical organizer for your favorite hard-or soft-covered books.

Only $9.95

Approximately 16" x 8" when assembled

Assembles in seconds!

To order, rush your name, address and zip code, along with a check or money order for $10.70* ($9.95 plus 75¢ postage and handling) payable to *Harlequin Reader Service*:

> Harlequin Reader Service
> Book Rack Offer
> 901 Fuhrmann Blvd.
> P.O. Box 1396
> Buffalo, NY 14269-1396

Offer not available in Canada.

*New York and Iowa residents add appropriate sales tax.

BKR-1A

Harlequin Presents

Coming Next Month

Available in December wherever paperback books are sold, or through Harlequin Reader Service:

In the U.S.
901 Fuhrmann Blvd.
P.O. Box 1397
Buffalo, N.Y. 14240-1397

In Canada
P.O. Box 603
Fort Erie, Ontario
L2A 5X3

**For the millions who can't read
Give the Gift of Literacy**

One out of five adults in North America
cannot read or write well enough
to fill out a job application
or understand the directions on a bottle of medicine.

**You can change all this by joining the fight
against illiteracy.**

For more information write to:
Contact, Box 81826, Lincoln, Neb. 68501
In the United States, call toll free: 1-800-228-8813

**The only degree you need
is a degree of caring**

LIT-A-1R

Six exciting series for you every month... from Harlequin

Harlequin Romance·
The series that started it all

Tender, captivating and heartwarming...
love stories that sweep you off to faraway places
and delight you with the magic of love.

◆

Harlequin Presents·
Powerful contemporary love stories...as individual as the women who read them

The No. 1 romance series...
exciting love stories for you, the woman of today...
a rare blend of passion and dramatic realism.

◆

Harlequin Superromance®
It's more than romance... it's Harlequin Superromance

A sophisticated, contemporary romance-fiction
series, providing you with a longer,
more involving read...a richer mix of complex plots,
realism and adventure.

Harlequin
American Romance™
Harlequin celebrates the American woman...

...by offering you romance stories written about American women, by American women for American women. This series offers you contemporary romances uniquely North American in flavor and appeal.

♦

Harlequin Temptation™
Passionate stories for today's woman

An exciting series of sensual, mature stories of love...dilemmas, choices, resolutions... all contemporary issues dealt with in a true-to-life fashion by some of your favorite authors.

♦

Harlequin Intrigue
Because romance can be quite an adventure

Harlequin Intrigue, an innovative series that blends the romance you expect... with the unexpected. Each story has an added element of intrigue that provides a new twist to the Harlequin tradition of romance excellence.

Harlequin Books™

PROD-A-2